A Wife

for

Carter

WENDY MAY ANDREWS

~~~

Sparrow Ink
www.sparrowink.com
~~~

ISBN - 978-1-989634-52-3

Cover Design by Les at *GermanCreative*

Photography by *Envision Literary Photography*

www.wendymayandrews.com

**They didn't meet until...
after the wedding day.**

Carter McLain has finally accomplished the success he was striving for when he moved to the frontier a decade ago. All that's missing is a wife to share it with. Having no desire to leave his land, he requests a friend back home to arrange a proxy marriage for him. When his bride seems too good to be true, Carter wonders if he did the right thing.

The highly publicized deaths of Ella St. Clair's parents cause her to lose everything. Left destitute, alone, and friendless, she grudgingly accepts the offer of marriage by proxy to a man she has never met. The long trip West leaves her plenty of time for second thoughts.

What does the future hold for these legally bound strangers? Can they get past their secrets to find happiness?

Dedication

In this book, Ella finds herself in a very tight spot in life and one of the things she misses most are her books. I can so relate to this sentiment. Whenever I need a break from life's tight spots, I find relief by reading a good book. When I get to the end, I'm refreshed and ready to figure my way out of the issue. I know I'm not alone in this. This book is for all those who use the same coping device.

And to my hubby for being there to help me figure life out.

Acknowledgements

Thanks go to my beta readers: Marlene, Suzanne, Christina, Monique, and Alfred – your zeal for my stories and making them better makes my heart happy.

Thank you to my editor, Julie Sherwood, I love working with you. Any mistakes left are my fault, not hers.

Thank you too to my online communities full of wonderful readers and writers who help me with research or cheer me on. I am constantly amazed by the human kindness that can still be found even online.

Special thanks to my parents for reading to me as a child and for always keeping me supplied with books, even when money didn't grow on trees. Those Scholastics flyers were SO exciting!

And sincere thanks need to also go to my husband for being my everything – friend, partner, companion, web guru, formatter, idea sounding board, counterpart. You're the best, Mr. Andrews.

Chapter One

Ella had to shade her eyes as she stepped down from the train car. She wouldn't have ever thought the sun was brighter in the west. She didn't think that was possible. But that's sure how it seemed. Looking around, her gaze flitted about like a nervous bird. Everyone was bustling by with somewhere to go, and her fellow passengers were eagerly being greeted. Ella expected there was someone waiting for her as well, but of course, she had no way of knowing who it was. Fred's description hadn't given her much to go on.

"I don't know. He's tall with brown hair," had been the answer when she had asked for a description of her husband. That described at least seventy-five percent of the men milling about. Ella wanted to giggle as that thought passed through her mind. She hoped that meant she had retained her sense of humor and not that she was losing her mind.

Grasping her baggage tightly, relieved for once at how little she owned, Ella resolved to find somewhere to sit and wait. Surely once the crowds cleared out, she'd be in a better position to figure out which one was her husband. *At least it doesn't stink here,* she thought as she made her way to a bench in the shade of the overhang along the front of the train station. *Or is it the back?* she questioned, maybe she ought to go to the other side where the horses and wagons would be. But it seemed everyone who had people waiting for them were being greeted on this side, the train side. *Stick with your first plan,* she admonished herself. *He'll find you eventually.*

After her trip, Ella was feeling hot and grubby. The gloves that had been pristine when she left Boston were now smudged, and she wondered if it would be better to meet her husband with bare hands or dirty gloves. Then she shook her head. It was a foolish thing to worry about. She wasn't in Boston anymore. And she had yet to meet her husband.

Her stomach ached from nerves and hunger, and she gnawed on her lip with worry. It was unfortunate that she hadn't been able to muster up the nerve to ask Fred for some spending money before he put her on the train. He had bought her ticket for her, but she hadn't felt right asking him for more than that. However, since she was out of money herself, that meant once her small supply of food had run out, there was nothing for her to eat. It had been two days, and she was feeling the effects. It was good that she was able to find a shady spot to sit; she didn't think she would have been able to bear up under the blazing sunshine if she had needed to remain standing there on the train platform.

As her stomach growled again, Ella felt a blush climbing in her cheeks. It was so loud that time, she was sure others could hear it. She sure hoped her new home wasn't overly far from the town. And that her husband had thought to stock up the larder. She simply wouldn't be able to manage much longer without something to eat.

Looking around, she could see that there were fewer people now. In fact, the platform was very nearly empty. Her gaze encountered the interested stare of what appeared to be a handsome cowboy. She almost became ensnared by his intense blue gaze, but she managed to move her eyes away and keep her composure. It would not do for her husband to arrive and find her ogling another man. Ella hoped her face wasn't flaming with awareness as she kept her gaze averted. She sighed. Surely her husband would arrive shortly. She had sent word of which train she was on. In fact, that was where she had spent her last coins, on sending the telegram at their last stop. Fred had told her to wait until the last day just in case there were delays. There hadn't been many delays, she was relieved to note. And it had only taken five days to get here from Boston. Train travel really was a modern marvel.

Ella could still feel the stare of the handsome stranger, and it made her want to fidget. She knew she must look a fright after five days on the train. There hadn't been much opportunity to wash or even change her clothes, so she must be looking much worse for the wear. But it was exceedingly rude of him to stare in such a way. It's not as though she had meant to be so frayed. If she had her wishes granted, she would be ravishingly beautiful when she met her husband for the first time. She almost grinned. Of course, if she had her 'druthers, she wouldn't have needed to wed a stranger in the first place. But beggars couldn't be choosers, and it was better than the alternative. At least she was protected now. And Fred had spoken so highly of this Carter McLain. She ought to be grateful for her circumstances. And she promised herself she would be as soon as he turned up. Surely she couldn't be expected to be extremely positive in the face of an empty train platform.

Ella sighed again. Standing up, she shook out her skirts and was about to hoist her suitcase up to traipse around to the other side of the station when a deep voice interrupted her thoughts over her right shoulder.

"Excuse me, ma'am, you wouldn't by any chance be Mrs. Ella McLain, would you?"

She nearly jumped out of her skin. Ella was weak with fatigue and hunger and was so caught up in her own dilemma that she hadn't expected anyone to speak to her so suddenly. With a slight shriek, she whirled around and almost toppled over.

The handsome cowboy was standing much too close, but at least that made it possible for him to catch her by the elbow before she actually took a tumble.

"Who are you?" she asked suspiciously, not answering his question.

He pulled off his hat, apparently remembering his manners, and replied, "I might be your husband," he answered with a grin. "I'm Carter McLain."

It was all too much for Ella. The heat, her hunger and lack of sleep on the noisy train, and now to discover the most handsome man she had ever seen was her new husband. Her legs gave out, and she wilted into a faint.

She wasn't to know how much time passed, but the next thing she knew she was back on the bench. Mortification assailed her as she realized what must have happened.

Well isn't that a fine introduction, she mused. *He's certainly going to think he's been saddled with a fine specimen.* Even in her mind her voice was dripping with sarcasm. The thought made her smile, which probably made her look even more a simpleton. The handsome man was hovering over her. His frown deepened as he observed her smile.

Yep, he definitely thinks he took the prize now, she thought again. *Probably thinks I've lost my mind. And maybe I have. What with marrying a stranger without even clapping eyes on him first.* Well, now she had seen him, and she was quite certain it was all a huge mistake. How could she bear to be married to such a gorgeous man? He'd surely have the ego to match, and she had experienced quite enough of that in her short life. She couldn't help but sigh.

"Are you feeling a little more like yourself, Miss?" The handsome man hovered over her and seemed genuinely concerned about her welfare. It was a pleasant thought. No one had truly cared about her in eons, it seemed. Sometimes she wondered if anyone ever had, but that was disloyal to her lovely parents. It wasn't their fault they hadn't been able to provide for her after their deaths. They had done the very best they could, she was sure.

"You must not be used to the heat, are you Miss?" His handsome face split into a grin, and she had to blink against the brilliance of it. "I guess I ought to be calling you ma'am now, if you truly are the one I'm waiting for."

Ella wasn't going to remain prostrate before her new husband for another minute. She did not want him settling into the impression that she was a weakling. While Fred had assured her their agreement was binding, she didn't want her new husband deciding he had changed his mind about her. She brushed the back of her hand over her forehead and instinctively flattened any stray hairs as she regained her feet as gracefully as she could with a large man leaning over her. She was certain he meant to be solicitous, but his towering was becoming slightly intimidating despite his pleasant smile.

"Yes, sir, I am Ella. And no, I'm not yet accustomed to the heat. I didn't really expect it to be that much hotter than it was in Boston. In the city, the air is already starting to cool, readying for winter. I guess it's the proximity to the ocean that makes it cooler."

She wasn't sure what to make of the fact that he just stood there gaping at her. Had she said something wrong?

"You are the prettiest little thing I've ever seen in these parts," he said. He sounded almost as though he were in awe of her, which was ridiculous.

She couldn't help it. A giggle escaped her. "You must not get out much, then, sir, but I thank you kindly for the compliment." She brushed it aside, not really believing him. "Now, I do apologize for fainting on you. I must assure you, it is not a regular occurrence for me. I am fit as a fiddle and will not be lazing about like a hot house flower. I just haven't had any breakfast yet today, so I was a little unprepared for the elements."

He kept grinning as he listened to her words. "You even sound pretty," he commented. "But if you're hungry, we'd best be getting you fed. It's a bit of a ride out to our place. I wouldn't want you fainting again from hunger and heat while we're driving."

"That's kind of you, sir, thank you."

"It's the very least I can do, since you've come all this way."

Ella felt some of her nerves loosen. Even though she could barely look at him for how handsome he was, the fact that Mr. McLain seemed to be kind and compassionate helped settle her a little more into the decision she had made. Not that she'd had much choice. The next step for her would have been the workhouse if she hadn't accepted the offer of an arranged marriage. But she was still left wondering why he had wanted such a match. If Fred were to be believed, her new husband was comfortably situated. And no woman would fault the man for his looks. So why had he felt it necessary to find himself a bride and marry her by proxy before he had even laid eyes on her? Ella would have to be subtle if she were going to discern the truth. In her experience, men didn't ever say straight what the situation was.

Just look at her and where she had found herself. Sibby's husband had sworn he would look after her. But it turned out it wasn't the kind of looking after she was interested in. And she could never confide that to Sibby, of course. What good would it do to break her best friend's heart? She was just glad that Sibby trusted her brother and what he had to say about the gentleman now before her. Then again, Sybil's judgment was not the most trustworthy when it came to men. She did marry Horace after all. But Ella trusted Fred and would have to trust this man, at least until he gave her reason not to.

"Is this all you've brought with you?" He seemed surprised by her meager baggage. Her cheeks warmed.

"I didn't want to be burdened with too much during all that travel," she murmured.

"Not to worry, we can send to have your things shipped on another train."

Ella couldn't look at him. Didn't he realize a woman who would agree to an arrangement like theirs didn't have an excess of belongings? She decided to leave the issue to be dealt with later.

She was glad she didn't have to carry anything, and she gingerly clung to the arm he offered. Ella had not expected to find a gentleman at the end of her journey. Her curiosity about this man mounted. What kind of man required a proxy bride? She had been expecting a rough outdoorsman with poor manners and missing teeth. Thus was the extent of her desperation to accept the offer. She didn't trust this apparent good fortune. There must be something she was missing, a salient fact that explained why an apparently well to do, handsome, well mannered man needed to have his friends arrange a marriage for him. She didn't think the fact that he was isolated could be the full explanation. Ella determined to remain on her guard. She just prayed he was nothing like Sybil's husband. Ella mustered up her courage. She would cross that bridge if she came to it.

Looking around at the small town as they walked toward the hotel with a restaurant in the front, Ella felt her confidence growing. *It really is almost a city,* she thought as she took in the store fronts and shops as they hurried along. Even though her new husband had been so solicitous of her, he clearly didn't realize his stride was much longer than hers. She had to almost run to keep up. *But at least I don't have to carry my baggage,* she reminded herself, trying to see the bright side of the situation. And living in a place like this wasn't going to be so very dreadful, she was beginning to think.

Once they had been seated at a table they were quickly served. The restaurant had a surprisingly detailed menu. Ella was afraid they might have been more glamorous in their descriptions than the food was going to prove to be, but she expected the food to be at least edible. The place appeared clean, and that was all she could hope for.

What does one discuss with one's husband that one has just met? Ella's thoughts again provided her with amusement, but she tried to keep it from showing on her face. She didn't want the man thinking she was an escaped lunatic. He must have already received a bad enough impression of her from her faint upon their first introduction. He didn't appear to be much of a talker given he hadn't said anything since they had left the train station. She really needed to bestir herself and find out a little bit about him before she accompanied him much further.

"Is your home very far from here?"

He blinked his bright blue eyes at her as though he were surprised by her question. She wondered if he had forgotten she was there. A smile spread across her face. She wouldn't really mind if he forgot about her as long as he provided her with a roof over her head and some food on the table.

"It's a little far. We'll actually be driving for a few hours in the wagon to get home."

"A few hours?" Ella tried not to sound dismayed. She had been excited by the thought of being so close to the town of Council Bluffs. "Is it very isolated where we're going?" Her heart gave a slight lurch at the thought of being secluded with the handsome stranger.

"Somewhat," was his uninformative reply. "Didn't Fred tell you I'm a rancher?"

Ella nodded. "He did. But he didn't have much more information than that, I'm afraid. So do you tend to stock up on your supplies only occasionally when you come up to Town?"

"I try to never come here if I can help it. I only came today because I didn't want you to have to worry about figuring out how to get to Traders Point."

Ella felt a degree of relief over his words. "Oh, and what is in Traders Point?"

"A few shops and a mercantile. We can get anything we can't make ourselves from there or have it ordered in for us. You won't find us so very backward, I can promise you that."

Ella knew her smile was weak but she gave it anyway. "It'll be fine. I tried to have as few preconceived notions as possible since I had very little information, but as we traveled from town to town on the train, I couldn't help imagining what it will be like."

"My land is extensive and productive," he said proudly. Ella wasn't sure exactly what that was in reply to so she just nodded and smiled.

"We don't lack for much," he added.

As if on cue, their food arrived. Ella tried not to devour it like the ravenous person she was, but she turned her attention to the food and gave up on trying to talk to the man at her side. Several minutes later, she could finally feel some relief from the deep hunger pangs, and she was able to look up from her plate. She was forced to blink. She hoped her cheeks weren't flaming but they probably were, she acknowledged, as she realized her handsome new husband was staring at her.

"You've certainly got a healthy appetite," he commented, a twitch of his lips showing he was trying not to laugh.

Ella wanted to crawl under the table and disappear, but that wasn't an option. She tried to be brave instead. "Like I mentioned, I was rather hungry."

"Well, I am relieved that we were able to alleviate your need for the moment," he replied, not appearing to have taken offense. "Please, don't stop unless you're finished."

Her appetite had fled by now, but she had learned the hard way not to pass up available food. Ella forced herself to finish the rest of her meal. It sat heavy in her stomach, but she ignored the discomfort. He had said it was a long way to his home, and she didn't want to be hungry along the way.

Before the silence became too dreadfully awkward, they were interrupted by a feminine voice from behind Ella's shoulder.

"Good morning, Mr. McLain. What a surprise meeting you in Council Bluffs today. I thought you never ventured past the village if there was not dire need."

Ella felt herself stiffen at the woman's tone, but she tried to keep her smile pleasant as she turned to see who was speaking in such a familiar way to Mr. McLain. When she then glanced at him, it was difficult to interpret his expression. It was a mixture of irritation and amusement. He obviously knew the woman. Ella shifted her gaze back to the nosy meddler.

The woman was rather mousy with small features and sandy brown hair, but she looked like she was trying to be a fashion plate. Ella was uncomfortable with the way the woman's eyes seemed to be cataloguing every aspect of her attire. She wished the woman had not intruded on their meal, but Ella had been raised a certain way so there was nothing to be done but to put out her hand and introduce herself.

"It's nice to meet you," she began, almost stuttering over the fact that she didn't know what to call herself. She skipped that part, hoping the woman wouldn't notice. She seemed to be full of her own importance so she might not much care for Ella's name.

The woman's handshake was limp, and her face looked as though she had sucked on a lemon as Mr. McLain stepped in to perform the introductions.

"Mrs. Crocker, this is my wife, I was just picking her up from the train."

The woman's eyes couldn't have gotten any rounder. "Are you a mail order bride then?" she demanded.

Ella felt her face heating. She coughed to cover her discomfort, and Mr. McLain covered over the awkward moment by interrupting. "What brings you to The Bluffs, Mrs. Crocker? Is Jacob with you?"

Mrs. Crocker appeared startled by the question, as though she had something to hide, but she recovered and made polite conversation briefly.

"It will be pleasant to have another woman close by. We're practically neighbors. I'm sure we'll run into each other from time to time."

Ella wasn't certain of the woman's sincerity, but she made an appropriate reply. Within moments Mrs. Crocker quickly made her excuses and left them. It had been a strange encounter but was soon forgotten.

Without much further ado, they finished their meal, Mr. McLain settled up their bill, and he ushered her from the room. Handing her up onto the wagon with one hand while tossing her baggage into the back with the other, the man displayed his strength in a magnificent way. Ella had to bite her lip and avert her gaze so as not to ogle him. She felt as though her temperature were rising. It was highly uncomfortable. How was she going to be able to bear living with the man?

As they set off, she noticed they were heading almost due south. She pondered over that realization, noting that had he lived further west, she could've gotten off at a later stop. The rancher didn't seem overly inclined to conversation, so Ella allowed her mind to wander back over how she had managed to find herself in her present circumstances.

Chapter Two

Boston 1866

"You want me to do what?" Ella must not have heard correctly.

"It isn't so very unreasonable, Ella," Sibby pointed out, sounding as though she were explaining something to a child. "Women agree to arranged marriages all the time. There are often ads in the newspaper from gentlemen seeking a wife."

"I know. I've seen the advertisements myself, but I never considered replying to one."

"Do you really have much other choice?"

Ella pondered the question but tried to ignore the truth of her friend's words. "Even a mail-order bride can change her mind if she reaches her destination and decides the man won't suit her. What your brother is suggesting will remove even that opportunity from me. Do you really think I'm that desperate?"

"Aren't you, my dear? You know Horace has tied my hands. I can't help you anymore. He wants you gone from the house and won't give me a single cent to help you."

"Not that I want you to give me your money, Sibby." Ella's reply was prompt and stiff before she ran across the room and flung herself to the floor by her friend's seat. Placing her head in Sibby's lap, Ella exclaimed softly, "I never meant to cause any trouble for you with your husband, my dear friend. I am so sorry that I have brought my problems into your home."

"Don't be silly," her friend reprimanded, even as she soothed her by stroking her unruly curls back from her brow. "I would do it every single day if the need arose. And I actually hate to push you into agreeing to Fred's proposition, since it will mean you will promptly move across the country. But I don't see very many other options for you. This proxy arrangement will be a protection for you. Yes, you won't be able to change your mind, but then neither will he be able to. Wouldn't it be terrible if you went all that way and then found out he had changed his mind? This way, if you're already legally wed, he is obliged to provide for you immediately."

Ella sighed. How had it come to this? She glanced down at her fashionable gown. Or rather, it was fashionable two years ago when she had arranged for it to be made. It had held up remarkably well under the strain of being worn well past its intended use. If only her parents hadn't died in such an unsavory manner, she wouldn't be broke and unmarriageable. Before their deaths, she had enjoyed the attentions of several suitors. However, as soon as word had gotten out what had happened to her parents, they had all disappeared from view. Not that she wanted any of them anyway. If they couldn't stand by her in her hour of need, they were of no use to her. But then, no one had stood by her except Sibby. Sybil Trenton, her friend from boarding school. They had been fast friends since they were little girls. And despite how silly Sybil might be at times, Ella would be eternally grateful for her loyal friendship. She would have been homeless these last few months if not for Sibby.

Another sigh escaped her. It would have been idyllic if not for Horace. Ella couldn't quite suppress her shudder. How did her lovely friend end up saddled with such a dreadful husband? And from thus stemmed the true reason for her hesitation in accepting Sibby and Fred's proposition. What if this unknown gentleman ended up being similar to Sybil's husband? She would be bound to him until death did them part. A large part of her would rather be in the workhouse. But the rest of her would prefer some semblance of the life she had known. She didn't know if she could survive the workhouse. She would like to think she could be a hard worker, but she had never done a day of manual labor in her life, so it was doubtful she could start doing it now. Of course, if she accepted this stranger's proposal and moved to his "spread," whatever that was, out West, she would obviously be expected to do a certain amount of work. He couldn't be expected to have servants to cater to her. But it wouldn't be like the workhouse. She had toured one before with her mother, when they were looking for the less fortunate to assist with their good works.

Ella almost snorted as she thought of it. They and all their friends had thought they were doing right by people. Feeling blessed in their own good fortune, they had wanted to help those worse off than they were. But here she was in desperate need, and none of those so called well-meaning women would even consider lifting a finger for her. But she was straying from her point, even if it were in her own mind. She had witnessed what the workhouses were like, and she knew she wouldn't be able to do it. And Sybil was correct, with absolutely no money of her own, Ella couldn't risk the precariousness of traveling out west as merely some man's intended. If she married him by proxy, he would be obligated to keep her. Even if he found out about her past.

And that was where the true rub came.

"What will I tell him?"

Sybil didn't even pretend to mistake her meaning. "You needn't give him every last detail. You have been orphaned and found yourself in straightened circumstances beyond your control. It is the absolute truth."

"It's true, but it's not all of it."

"What are the chances that he'll be finding out the whole story from someone else? You know full well, no one from our circles will be traveling west any time soon."

"Not even you?" Ella could hear how small her voice sounded and grimaced. There was nothing left for her here in Boston, but she couldn't bear the thought of never again seeing the only friend she had left in the world.

"I hope, once he's gotten over his irritation with me, Horace will allow me to visit you eventually, but that is hardly the point."

Ella couldn't help grinning. Her sense of humor was the only thing that had saved her these past months. She managed to find the humor in everything. Not everyone appreciated that skill, but it had preserved her senses while everything she knew had been stripped from her.

She just hoped Sybil would be able to visit her one day, preferably without her lecherous husband. She could do without the experience of keeping him at arm's length. It was the silver lining of being put from the house. At least now she no longer had to avoid his advances while simultaneously keeping Sybil unaware of his unsavory inclinations. Not that she really believed Sybil was fully unaware, but it would hurt her to know he had directed his attentions at her dearest friend.

"I know, and you're right, it is doubtful anyone will be visiting. But we know so little of this man. Isn't there a chance he has family around here that might fill him in on the details?"

"It'll be too late by then, and you will no longer be Ella St. Clair anyway, so what will it matter?"

"I could consider that I should be grateful for the fact that society has known me as Eleanor, instead of Ella. That might help. I will be Ella McLain in the future, and poor Eleanor St. Clair's trials needn't affect me at all."

"That's the spirit. So you will accept, then?"

Ella heaved another heartfelt sigh. "As you said, I haven't much other choice."

From that moment on, it was all a blur. The maids were set to packing Ella's few possessions. She did have several gowns that were still holding up, but Ella questioned how much use they would be for her out West. She rather suspected she would need sturdier clothing in her future. But she would cross that bridge when she reached it, she reminded herself. Luckily for her, every well born lady was taught to do needlework. Surely sewing some garments wouldn't be all that difficult. If one could monogram handkerchiefs, surely one could make a gown. Her lips twisted in wry amusement. She doubted it would be that simple, but she refused to think she wasn't up to the challenge. She reminded herself once more that it would surely be better than slaving in the workhouse.

The vows she exchanged with Fred as proxy felt meaningless, but Ella knew they were legally binding. She tried to appreciate Fred's cooperation in the arrangements. As Sybil's brother, he obviously felt a sense of responsibility toward his sister's friend. It was the only reason he would consider Ella for the arrangement.

"I know what happened to your parents wasn't your fault, Miss Eleanor, so I don't mind so much letting you into this arrangement. You better not make me regret it. I have my reputation to uphold."

Ella's smile had been stiff as she had accepted the slight insult.

"I realize you're doing me a favor, but if you do not feel that you can trust me, perhaps you ought to do your friend out West a favor and not perform this arrangement."

While she had kept her tone pleasant, it must have been apparent that he had been offensive. "I apologize, Miss St. Clair, I did not mean you any disrespect. Of course, I trust you. I trust the both of you. I have every expectation that Carter will make you a fine husband."

Ella wished in that moment, so fiercely that she could feel it down to her toes, that she were not in this mess. That her parents were still alive, that she was oblivious to the shallowness of all the relationships in her life, except for Sybil, of course. She wished too that she was at home, curled up in the window seat with a purring cat in her lap without a single care in all the world. Ella would never take that life for granted ever again, if she could only have it back. With a deep sigh, she acknowledged that wishes don't come true. This was the hand life had dealt her, and she needed to accept it with as much grace as she could muster.

She offered Fred as warm a smile as she could manage. "I appreciate your help in arranging my affairs, Fred, and I assure you, you will have no reason to regret it on my account."

Fred, always the jovial sport, couldn't hold on to any stiffness and seemed relieved that she wasn't going to hold a grudge.

"I would say anytime, but hopefully you'll never have need of any assistance again."

"That is the dream," Ella replied with a soft smile, unwilling to accept that there were no dreams left for her. Suddenly she had to laugh. She was being melodramatic, and it was doing no one any good.

"Very well, Fred, what do we do now?"

"We've just signed all the necessary paperwork. If you're packed up, I can get you on the first train headed West in the morning."

Ella blinked. There was to be no time for second thoughts. Just as well. Second, even third, thoughts would do her little good. She should be relieved there would be no delay in getting on with it. Any delay would have only left her time to fret. She nodded and forced more warmth into her smile as she thanked her friend's brother.

"I appreciate your attention to all the details."

Sybil had been silent throughout the exchange, but she now surged to her feet. Her eyes were swimming in tears, but she had a smile on her face.

"Oh, my dearest friend, I don't know if I'm happy or sad in this moment. I'm thrilled that you are situated. Fred has assured me that this fellow is a kind gentleman who will treat you well. But oh, how I wish there was no need for you to go."

Ella pulled her weeping friend into her arms. "As do I, of course, but there's nothing to be done about it. And now I'm to have an adventure. Just think of the letters I'll be able to send."

A watery chuckle was her answer before Sybil pulled her head up. "How do you always manage to be so cheery? If you weren't my friend, I would find it to be a rather disturbing trait."

Ella grinned in reply and just offered a shrug. What was there to say? It was the only way she could cope.

~~~

It was a bright, warm, end of summer day as she climbed up into the train. Fred had arranged her passage, and she trusted the ride would be as painless as possible. They were not early for the train, for which Ella was grateful. There was only time to hand up her luggage and hug Sybil once more before she was being urged to hurry as the train was about to depart. As she stepped up into the car, it began to move. She waved frantically to her only loved one remaining on earth and tried to stem the flow of her tears.

Her tears had long since dried now. Boredom and frustration had set in long before she had reached her destination. She was hungry, dishevelled, and soot stained from the days on the coal-powered conveyance. But she was alive and free from the burdens that had assailed her in Boston. It had to be uphill from here, she assured herself. She would make it so. Surely she was capable of making her life into a success despite the recent disasters. Fred, for all his foppish ways, surely wouldn't send her into a bad situation.

She determined that she would be a successful wife of someone who owned a "spread." She really ought to have asked Fred what that meant. She didn't want to appear ignorant in front of her new husband. Of course, that was going to be impossible to avoid considering she really knew nothing of use. She had been raised to be a matron
~~~

of high society. But thankfully, she had also been raised to use her keen mind and understanding. So hopefully that would kick in at some point. The thought amused her and Ella was able to put a smile on her face as she stepped down from the train at the end of the line. If she had wanted to go any further, she would need another ticket and would have to change rail companies.

Council Bluffs was an odd name for a town, but she was happy to have finally reached it. At least she was mostly happy. Part of her was enjoying the limbo she had been living in for the past few days as she rode the train West. No one knew her. No one had any preconceived notions or expectations of her. And she didn't yet have to face her new husband. But she couldn't remain in limbo any longer. She was here now and had to face the future.

Chapter Three

Carter could hardly believe how lovely his wife was. He hadn't identified himself to her when she first exited the train because he was certain she couldn't be the one he was waiting for. But when no other unaccompanied females exited the train, he had approached her, assuming that either his wife had been delayed somewhere along the way or this was, indeed, her.

And her it was. He couldn't believe his good fortune. She seemed reasonably good humored, at least passably intelligent, and was the prettiest little thing he'd laid his eyes on in the past several years. Maybe ever, but he couldn't really recall. Of course, there was that little incident of her fainting. He truly hoped she wasn't a sickly sort, as she wouldn't hold up very well out on their spread. Not that they were so very far from civilization, but he was counting on a wife who could do at least a little bit more than just look pretty.

As they left the town behind, Carter was able to allow his mind to wander, since the horses could practically drive themselves over the familiar road.

He was glad the woman, his new wife, he reminded himself, wasn't a chatterbox. The more he thought about what a pretty picture she was, the happier he became with her arrival. Especially if one contrasted her with the wife poor Jacob Crocker got, Carter realized he had gotten the luck of the draw. Really, she was so lovely, it wouldn't matter so much if she wasn't of much use on the spread. In all reality, Carter had the resources; if he needed to hire more help, he could. He was just happy to have a companion. And he really liked that she seemed to be cheerful despite the little awkwardness at the beginning when she had fainted. Her robust appetite certainly must prove she wasn't the sickly sort. It must've been the heat, like she said, added to her hunger. The more he thought about it, the harder his heart began to pound. *I'm going to love this woman,* he thought as a giddy feeling welled in his chest.

But as he sat there cataloguing her virtues while she merely gazed about taking in the scenery, he started to become a little suspicious. Why would such a paragon accept an arrangement such as they had made? What wasn't she telling him? Was she perhaps out to swindle him in some way?

Carter's mouth went dry at the thought that he might have saddled himself with a criminal or some sort of ne'er-do-well. His brother had warned him. He should have bestirred himself and gone back East to find himself his own bride. But Carter hadn't wanted to go to the bother. And for that he might pay dearly. His brother had also suggested Carter ought to at least send for her without marrying her in advance, but he didn't want to take the risk of her coming all this way and changing her mind like had happened to Sammy Smith last year. Those mail order brides weren't always trustworthy, either. He figured if the woman was willing to say her vows, she was fully committed to sharing his life. But now he was beginning to wonder how this beautiful woman could have possibly had circumstances that made their arrangement the best option for her.

He really ought to ask her some questions. He had gotten used to the silence of living alone and so had to think rather harder than he should have needed to in order to come up with appropriate and acceptable questions.

He cleared his throat before speaking, which caused Ella's direct, green gaze to collide with his. This caused him to stall on her appearance once more. She had unusual coloring. Dark hair with green eyes. He would have thought her eyes would match more with red hair. His focus centered on her head for a pace while he wondered if she had colored her hair. He didn't know how anyone could achieve that color and have it look so real, but he supposed it was possible. What did he know about the wiles of women?

She was still looking at him expectantly, so Carter finally launched into his question after clearing his throat again. "So, were you always the adventurous sort?"

She answered him with a trill of laughter, kind of like the sound a lively bird might make, he thought fancifully. "I would rather describe myself as the least adventurous soul you might meet, to be frank."

"I find that hard to believe," he remarked. He regretted his words when he saw how flustered it made her. She flushed up to the roots of her dark hair and looked away from him, as though she wanted to ignore his presence.

Carter cleared his throat again. "I meant you no insult, ma'am, I merely meant that getting on a westbound train, alone, to meet your new husband *after* you've said your vows seems to require a certain sense of adventure."

She trilled a laugh again, although this time it seemed a little less spirited. At least it didn't seem that she held a grudge toward him for his thoughtless words. "I guess I can see why you would think so, but I have to say, this is the first adventure I've taken."

"Are you going to be seeking out more adventures after this?"

"I suppose that remains to be seen, sir. I haven't yet seen how this one has turned out."

She sounded to him as though she were still deciding if he passed muster. Carter wasn't sure how he was feeling in that moment. Her being so pretty had thrown him completely. Not that he was being shallow. He had just been expecting a woman who was more desperate and therefore would be appreciative of what he had to offer. This beautiful woman must have had her choice of options. What if he couldn't keep her satisfied on his spread and she decided to leave him? Being legally bound to her would complicate both of their lives if he couldn't make her stay.

Carter vowed to do his best. But that still didn't mean he could trust her. And he definitely had no intention of giving her his heart just yet. He simply needed help and a companion. And eventually children would be nice.

Clearing his throat again, Carter ventured to address that sticky issue. "So, since we have just met, you are probably a little bit uncomfortable about us being alone together, am I right?"

He was surprised by the sunny smile she offered him at this question. "You are absolutely correct, but I hadn't wanted to bring it up."

He chuckled. He could feel his own face heating, but he persisted with his train of thought. "Well, I was thinking that we ought to give ourselves a little bit of time before we venture into an intimate relationship. Do you think we should set a time period, or just wait until we feel the timing is right?"

Carter watched in fascination as she seemed to take a large gulp at the question, but she kept a smile stretching her lips. He wondered if her smiles and laughter were actually a mask for her true feelings.

"I think a time period might be appropriate. If we left it until we feel it's right, we might never agree on that." The giggle that accompanied her words had an air of nervousness attached to it, but Carter couldn't help smiling along with her words.

"Do you think three months might be appropriate?" he asked, solicitous of her thoughts.

She blinked and her smile dimmed, but she didn't reveal her feelings. "Yes, that would probably be appropriate," she answered.

Carter was filled with relief. He was glad she seemed so amenable. Setting a limit on their celibacy would make it bearable and give him time to decide if he trusted her or not. Really, how could you be intimate with someone you didn't trust?

While he had become quite used to not having conversation going on around himself, he tried to exert himself to entertain her as they made the long drive home by pointing out various sights to her along the way. She seemed to be in awe of the scenery, which moved him to ask: "Have you never been outside of Boston before?"

"Not even once." Her reply was cheerful. "Although we would go to the beach on occasion, but it was practically within the city."

"Were you not nervous of leaving the city behind?"

"Not at all." The smile that accompanied this declaration appeared genuine and true. He wondered if she would elaborate. He waited a while to see if she would. Finally she spoke again. "While it will be an adjustment to get used to living far from conveniences like shops, I am looking forward to the challenge. And so far, everything I've seen has been beautiful. I look forward to learning everything I need to know."

This brought him to another concern.

"What do you know so far?"

He was intrigued by the expression that crossed her face. It seemed to be a mixture of uncertainty, embarrassment, and chagrin. But it was wiped away almost immediately by a wide grin, and she cheerfully pronounced, "Pretty much nothing of use, I'm afraid. I was raised to be a socialite. I can run a household of staff but have not done a single minute of manual labor in my entire life." She paused while that same expression shimmied across her face. She replaced her grin and continued, her tone full of determination. "But one thing I most certainly am not is stupid. I can be a hard worker, and I can learn."

Carter gulped. He should have written a few more requirements in his request to his friend Fred when he was asking him to arrange a wife for him.

"Well, we have a bit more of a drive. Is there anything you'd like to ask me?"

His pretty bride blinked at him and looked to be momentarily at a loss for words. Again a wide smile split her face. "I don't even know where to start!" She paused in thought before blurting her first question. "What's a spread?"

Carter wrinkled his brow in a frown, wondering what she was asking, but then his own face split in a grin. "My spread!" He laughed. "That's what we call a large piece of land upon which a man farms or raises cattle. In my case, I'm a rancher and we have quite a large spread for our cattle to roam around. In certain ways it's easier than farming. We only need to raise enough crops to feed ourselves and some for the animals through the winter in case it's a hard one."

"Are there different kinds of winters?" She seemed puzzled by his statement.

"Some years there's more snow than others, or the temperatures are lower than usual. When that happens, it's harder for the animals to look after themselves. And of course, we keep a few cows and chickens for our own milk and eggs, as well as meat, so they, being much more domesticated, need to be fed year round."

Her forehead creased in concentration. Carter thought it was adorable. He bit the inside of his cheek to stem his reaction. "You look confused."

She cocked her head. "So, do you mean some people raise a lot more crops than you do but fewer animals? And that's why you're a rancher instead of a farmer?"

"That's right." He nodded, pleased to see that despite her lack of knowledge, she wasn't a dimwit.

"Do you suppose one is less work than the other?" she asked, her forehead still creased in contemplation.

"I much prefer being able to roam freely over my land, not being tied quite so tightly to working the land. Of course, like I said, some has to be done for our own use, but that isn't the source of my income."

"So there's profit in farming and in ranching?"

"Most definitely, otherwise, why do it?"

She offered him half a smile and half a shrug, as though she hadn't even understood her own question. "I guess I figured it was just a means of survival."

"It is that, of course, and many just stop at that, but I don't aim to just be satisfied with mere survival. If my children don't want to follow in my footsteps, I want to be in a position to help them out with whatever they want to do. And if my wife wants new whatever, I want to be able to provide it. I want more."

He felt his face heat in response to her obvious embarrassment over his mention of buying his wife things. But he had no intention of withdrawing his words. If she stuck around and proved to be a halfway decent partner, he had every intention of treating her as well as he possibly could. He never wanted a woman of his to have to work herself to the bone like his mother had. He was going to make sure she had nice things and was satisfied with the bargain they had struck.

"Do you intend to live on your spread for the rest of your life?"

He was taken aback by her next tentative question.

"Are you pining for Boston already?"

"Not even a little bit." Her answer was quick and sounded sincere.

"Then why are you asking?"

She offered him another half shrug. "Your determination to turn a profit with your ranching reminds me of gentlemen in the city. So I thought you might be aspiring to return to prove a point of some sort."

Carter felt his respect for her grow, even as his suspicions mounted. She was far from dimwitted.

"I love life out here. I loved it when I first arrived, and it was as wild as can be. Now with the trains coming through, civilization is quickly trying to catch up to us. I love that civilization is within reach, but that I can stay far away from it if I wish. My land is extensive, as I mentioned, so I don't have to be concerned about being crowded out. But I don't see myself ever returning to live in Boston or anywhere else, for that matter." He stopped talking and glanced at her, wondering how she was receiving his words. He was surprised to see that she was merely nodding and listening with an attentive face. He added, "Of course, I might be willing to visit at some point."

This caused worry to spread across her face. "Won't that be a problem for the animals?"

"I have hands that can stay behind and look after things."

She wrinkled her nose and stared pointedly at his gloved hands that were holding the reins. Carter burst into laughter.

"Not my literal hands. A ranch hand is a hired helper who works on the land along with me."

"Oh!" she exclaimed then joined him in laughter. "I guess I have a lot to learn. Are you going to be terribly impatient with explaining everything to me?"

"I don't expect so." He answered as honestly as he could. "We've managed this long without you. We should be able to manage while you figure things out."

"Will you be able to spare the time to teach me whatever I need to know?"

"I had expected having a wife would require a certain amount of my time and attention, so I've accounted for it. The timing of your arrival is fortuitous, to be honest. Since it's almost fall, most of the harvest has already been done. The only truly pressing thing that needs to be finished before winter is to ride out and examine the entire fence line to ensure none of the animals will be going astray through the winter. And, ideally, to bring them in closer before winter closes in. We can't say for certain how hard or long the winter will be. It's better if the cattle are within easy range so we can check on them from time to time and make sure if they need to be provided any help or extra food."

"How many animals do you have?"

"A couple thousand. I don't know the exact number. We've had a number of births lately."

"A couple thousand?" She sounded incredulous. "That must be an awful lot of work to look after them all."

"Like I said, they're easier than raising crops for sale," he answered with a shrug.

"But what do you do with them? Sell them? Who would buy them? And especially at that volume? Doesn't everyone around here have cows of their own?"

Carter grinned. It was an intelligent question. And he was proud to be able to provide the answer. "With the train coming through regular like, we can actually sell to buyers from anywhere. Our hides are particularly wanted, especially by factories in the East."

He wasn't quite sure why she shuddered, but she kept a smile on her face throughout his explanation. So she couldn't be too uncomfortable with his words. Perhaps she was getting cold. Carter glanced at the sky. They had plenty of daylight left and the temperature hadn't dipped. Perhaps she was still unwell from her faint earlier.

Chapter Four

I f she hadn't accepted Fred's offer of marrying Carter McLain by proxy, Ella could have found herself working with his hides in a workhouse. The establishment she had toured back in Boston, was, from what she could tell, one of the least awful of the workhouses in the industrial part of the city. But it was a workhouse none the less.

She struggled to control her reaction to Carter's words and just barely managed not to gasp over his description of his business.

"You must be very industrious to have so many animals at this point. You don't look to be too terribly old." Ella felt her face flame over her words. Was it a terribly rude thing to say?

The deep chuckle of the handsome man at her side made her innards clench. She wasn't sure if it was a pleasant sensation. In fact, she rather thought it wasn't. She didn't want to feel attracted to him. She couldn't relax until she knew more about him. Yes, she had agreed to be his wife, but that didn't mean she had to let her feelings get wrapped up into the situation. That would just turn it into a fine mess, to be sure. She had to keep her wits about her. But she could be grateful that she would be seeing his animals while they were alive, rather than working with their hides in a factory as he had called it.

"No, I'm not terribly old. I just turned thirty."

"How did you get so much land and so many animals? Did you inherit the land from someone?"

"Nope. I worked for it. I've been out in these parts for more than twelve years. I grew up in Boston but couldn't bear to go into trade with my father, which is why I'm sensitive to the fact that my sons might not want to follow in my footsteps."

Ella was surprised that he was telling her so much. Over lunch, he had barely said five words to her, merely watching her in fascination as she ate her food. It had made her so uncomfortable. She felt like a specimen he was observing. She had been mortified. At least he didn't seem to have taken a disgust of her as he was suddenly much more talkative. Perhaps he was just uncomfortable in the town since, as he said, he's been out here in the wilderness for twelve years. He could just be unused to more people.

The drive was passing quickly and Ella was enjoying the scenery. It was more picturesque than some of what she had passed through while traveling on the train. Even though she had never been outside of Boston before, she was finding she quite liked the wildness of the place. She hoped, as he had said, that civilization didn't encroach too much on this beautiful, wild place.

"It should just be another half an hour or so." Her new husband spoke up after a bit of silence had stretched between them.

Ella smiled at him in thanks for the information but didn't comment. There didn't seem much to say to that. But he wasn't finished, it would seem. He cleared his throat.

"Do you cook?"

Feeling heat creep into her cheeks, Ella looked at him to gauge his reaction to her words. "A little," she answered.

He didn't say anything in response, merely nodding in acknowledgement.

Ella was left wondering what that meant. She had anticipated that she would need to prepare the meals so she had asked Sybil's cook to teach her as much as she could in the couple of days she was there after Horace had made it clear she was no longer welcome in their home. Right at that moment, everything the cook had taught her felt muddled up in her mind, but Ella was reasonably sure she would be able to manage at least some basic things.

"Perhaps we can work on it together for a couple of days until you're settled." He finally responded. Ella wondered what he was really feeling. She hadn't been watching him because she was too mortified and feeling insecure.

She nodded, still unable to look him in the eye. "That would be helpful, thank you."

"One of the hands might've gotten lunch started anyway before we arrive, so that will make tonight easier. If not, we'll just scrape something together as quickly as we can manage."

Again, Ella didn't have anything to add to his words. What was there to say, really? She was entering his life and his routine. She would adjust as well as she could manage. Hopefully she would prove to be an asset to his life rather than a burden. She was working on cultivating an attitude of gratitude. It helped keep her mind off all her complaints.

Turning her attention back to the scenery, Ella started her list for the day. *I'm grateful to be off the train. I'm grateful to finally have food in my stomach. I'm grateful for the blue sky. Can you imagine if it was raining? That would have been dreadful.* She dragged her straying attention back to the task at hand. *I'm grateful that my husband has all his teeth and seems to be a reasonable, intelligent man.* Even though Fred had assured her he was, she hadn't known what to expect. *I cannot say I'm grateful for how handsome he is, though. Although perhaps I should be grateful for that. It means, when we have children, they are far less likely to be teased for their appearance.*

Ella sighed. She had strayed from the topic once more. Well, at least she was grateful for a few things. She thought more about the conversation they had already shared. Since he had said that the arrival of winter was unpredictable in these parts, perhaps she should add to her list gratitude that it hadn't yet arrived. She was grateful that the sun was still high in the sky and providing enough warmth that she didn't have to shiver here next to the handsome stranger. That would have been the seal on her misery.

Ella dragged her thoughts back into control. *I'm a positive person, not a complainer*, she reminded herself. *I am not miserable. I am on an adventure. The sky is blue, the trees are green, the road isn't nearly as bumpy as I would have expected. I'll be able to walk around free of any encumbrance very soon. I will be safe, sound, and fed. What is there to complain about?*

She put on a wide smile and turned her focus back to the man at her side. "Do you have any pets?"

"Pets?" He repeated the word as though he didn't quite know what she meant.

She blinked at him. "Yes, you know, like animals you have no intention of selling or eating? And that don't need to work for you?"

The man grinned. "You really are city folk, aren't you?"

Ella felt hot color flood her cheeks. She surmised it was a stupid question to ask. But she had always wanted a pet. Her mother hadn't wanted animals in the house, and her father hadn't gainsaid her. Her imaginary fantasies about her life always included a cat in her lap and a dog at her feet.

"What kind of animal would you consider to be a pet?" he asked, sounding contrite, as though he hadn't meant to laugh at her. She felt a little bit better at this and tried to answer his question.

"Anything, really. Well, I guess it would have to be willing to be a pet, so probably a wild animal wouldn't do. I was hoping for a dog or a cat."

It was as though he couldn't help the guffaw that erupted from him because he looked immediately apologetic. "We have lots of cats. Every barn has cats. They keep the mouse population down."

"You have mice?"

He laughed again. She was getting used to the heat in her cheeks.

"I mentioned the food we have to keep in case it's a bad winter, right?"

She nodded.

"The mice love that food."

Ella hoped she didn't look too mortified at the thought of the mice. She knew they were a fact of life, but her mother had been obsessive about keeping every possible entry point sealed against the intrusion of any rodents. In Boston there were rats. She tried to imagine that mice weren't nearly so bad as rats. They were smaller at least. She brightened. At least they provided food for the cats.

"Do you think one of the cats would be interested in moving in with me?"

Carter stared at her for a moment, as though he were struck by her words. Ella couldn't imagine what there was to flummox him about her question.

"It might be best if you wait until there's a litter of kittens," he finally answered. "The grown cats might not be so keen on a life indoors, but if you get one young enough, it would probably grow accustomed."

Ella felt her face fall. "You don't think a cat would like to live indoors, do you?"

Carter shrugged. "Probably a kitten would love it. We'll see as soon as there's a litter, I promise. Might not be until spring though." There was another space of silence, and Ella tried not to be disappointed. At least he hadn't said she couldn't have a pet. He just hadn't expected such a question. Well, just as there were bound to be a million things Ella would have to get used to about her new life here in Iowa, surely it was only fair for him to get used to a few things, too.

"We do have dogs, but they work, so I don't think you'd consider them pets."

Ella brightened immediately. "Do they bite?"

"No," he sounded offended by the question. "At least, not people. I've trained them better than that."

"Sorry, I didn't mean the question to be offensive. I was just wondering if I could pet them."

"You could certainly try, if you want to. They can be awfully smelly sometimes."

Ella felt like singing. She was going to have pets. If she had to wait until spring for a kitten, that was fine by her. But there were dogs, and she was determined to make friends with them. This idea was looking better and better the further they got from the train. She took a deep, fortifying breath and decided she was going to make this situation work. The air was clean, the sky was blue, and the gossips of Boston were far behind her. It was going to be lovely; she just knew it. Just because she barely knew anything about anything useful wasn't a reason to quibble.

Chapter Five

Carter was stunned by the sunny smile his wife was wearing. At least this time it appeared to be truly genuine. He wondered what was traipsing through her head. Who knew what other ideas she was going to come up with? Not that he really minded the thought of having a cat in the house, he supposed. It would keep any mice out of the larder, too, which couldn't be a bad thing. And if she truly wanted one, what harm could it do? As long as she made sure it didn't have fleas. That would be dreadful. He'd worry about it when there was a litter, as he promised her. He was certain none of the barn cats would take kindly to being domesticated.

The drive home was beginning to wear on him. He wanted to get back home, get her settled in, and get back to his routine. While he was enjoying chatting with her far more than he would have expected, he was used to the silent contemplation the long drive usually afforded him. Now he found his head was filled with visions of his beautiful companion cuddling an armload of kittens, and while it was enchanting, he had no intention of being enchanted.

He studiously diverted his attention away from the distracting woman by his side. He needed to make sure his foreman had the men ready to ride out to round up the herd in the furthest fields. Carter supposed he shouldn't leave her alone right away, so he better not go until tomorrow. Make it the day after. He huffed a breath. Trying to think of something else didn't last long.

"Are you all right?" Her concerned question grated on his nerves.

"Never better," he replied with what he was sure was a fake looking smile. His tone didn't help much either. He didn't like the frown that was wiping out what seemed to be her perpetual smile.

After examining him with eyes that seemed to have seen more than she should have at her young age, she turned away and seemed to be studying the passing scenery once more. She didn't say anything more. Carter felt as though he had kicked one of the kittens she was determined to have. He sighed again. This was not the uncomplicated arrangement he had been hoping for. Already he was getting his feelings all tied up into the thing. That was the whole reason he had made such an arrangement. He didn't want any feelings.

Gritting his teeth when they hit a rut because he had allowed his attention to be diverted, Carter fixed his attention and his gaze back on the road ahead. The horses were picking up their pace. They could tell they were nearly home. He had never been happier to see the smoke emerging from behind the treeline that indicated the fire he had left banked in the kitchen was still burning. They were almost there.

Carter realized he ought to be thinking of her as more than "she" even in his head and would need to address her as something. He cleared his throat once more.

"Would you prefer I call you ma'am, Mrs. McLain, or Eleanor?"

The expression on her face was comical. It was as though she couldn't decide whether she was outraged or amused by his question.

"Would you really call me ma'am regularly?" She must have decided on amusement as he could hear laughter lurking in her tone.

"If that's what you would prefer."

"If you're giving me a choice, I would prefer none of those, thank you. My friends call me Ella."

"Really? Is there a reason?"

"Eleanor is what my parents called me when I was in trouble as a child. It cultivated a powerful dislike in me, as I'm sure you can imagine. And I'm afraid if you tried to call me Mrs. McLain, it might take me a while to realize that you were speaking to me, as it still doesn't feel real. Ella would be much more enjoyable for all of us."

"Then Ella it is," he agreed promptly before thinking of another problem. "I might not want the hands being familiar with you, though, so if you don't mind, I will direct them to call you Mrs. McLain or ma'am."

"If that's what you think is best."

He was feeling ridiculously puffed up by her quick acquiescence. He shook his head. He was losing his mind already.

To distract himself, he pointed out to her how close they were to their destination.

"Do you see that smoke curling out over the trees yonder?"

She followed his outstretched arm with her gaze, squinting in concentration.

"It looks kind of like clouds drifting through the air. Is that what you mean?"

"Yes, it isn't clouds though. Clouds are a different color and texture. That's the smoke from our chimney. We're almost there."

She bounced in her seat like a three-year-old and turned to him with shining eyes and a wide smile. "That drive wasn't nearly as bad as I thought it would be when you said it was a few hours. But I didn't see the village. Did I blink and miss it?"

He laughed. "No, we bypassed it. I was afraid you would want to stop, and I really wanted to get home before it got anywhere near dark."

She blinked, looking confused. Her lips parted as though she were going to comment, but she finally held her silence, merely nodding in acceptance of his statement. Her smile had dimmed, though, as she commented, "I'm glad we're almost there."

Carter again felt as though he had hurt her feelings somehow, but he wasn't sure what he had said wrong. He probably shouldn't have admitted that he didn't want to show her the village, but really, they had to get home, so what was he supposed to do? This having a wife business was far more complicated than he had expected.

Nothing more was said as they finally pulled into the lane leading up to his house. His chest filled anew with pride as he surveyed all that was his. He had only sent for a wife when he felt confident that he had a home to share with a family. When the final nail was set in his proper house he had written to Fred. Now it felt to him as though it glistened in the sun as it awaited his new wife.

Behind, and a little to the side of the new house, was the original shack he had erected on his property. It was where his ranch hands lived now — they were glad to be out of the hayloft of the barn. So everyone was happy. He glanced at the silent woman at his side. He was suitably satisfied by her wide eyes and gentle smile. She didn't have anything to say, but he felt she was impressed with what he could provide for her.

Carter hopped down from the wagon and hurried around to help his wife climb down. It was a good thing he was there as she was too busy looking around to pay close attention to what she was doing and she nearly fell out of the wagon.

"Whoopsy!" she said with laughter. "I guess I wasn't looking. Sorry 'bout that. I'm not usually quite this clumsy."

He found her delightfully charming but tried to ignore the sensation as he set her on her feet.

"I'll show you around a little bit before I put away the wagon."

"Thank you, that would be lovely."

He pointed out the barn and the various outbuildings as they walked to the house. After she climbed the two stairs to the porch, he opened the door with a flourish and a bow, making her giggle again. She sure was a cheerful little thing, he thought as his stomach and teeth clenched simultaneously.

The main floor was fairly simple, but he was proud of the large, spacious rooms. It was really not much more than one room, really, aside from the larder, but it was large, and it was his. The kitchen area took up the entire back half of the house with the larder on the side. The front door, being in the middle, separated the dining area from the sitting area in the front half of the house. It would be the perfect space for a large family or for hosting guests. Off to the side were the stairs leading up to four bedrooms. He was optimistic about the growth of his family.

Carter was waiting for her to say something. He couldn't tell what she was thinking from her face, as all he could see was her perpetually placed smile. Finally she met his gaze and gave her opinion.

"It's lovely and spacious. All the wood looks quite fresh, have you just built?"

"That's right. The house in the back where the hands live used to be my house."

"It seems you've been doing quite well for yourself, then," she added with a nod.

Carter was a little disappointed. There was less admiration in her tone than he would have liked to hear. Then he remembered that there were, of course, far grander homes in Boston, but surely she didn't come from one of those if she was here with him. He shook his head and excused himself.

"I'll just go see to the horses. Look around and make yourself feel at home. I'll bring your luggage in when I return."

"Thank you." She answered simply without looking at him again.

~~~

"I don't know what to make of her, Brent."

Carter was rubbing down one horse while his foreman was looking after the other. The horses were busily eating their feed and flicking their ears around in appreciation of the gentle brush strokes they were receiving.

"What do you mean, McLain?"

"I thought I was ready and even eager to have a woman in my home, but now I'm getting all squeamish at the last minute."

"So then, you don't know what to make of yourself, seems to me," the other man offered with a chuckle.

Carter laughed along with him. It was a reasonable observation.

"All she does is smile, but half the time it doesn't feel sincere. Even though I sent for her, I find myself wondering what kind of a woman would accept the arrangement I offered. She seems too well spoken and her clothes are too fancy for someone needing an arranged marriage."

"People fall on hard times all the time," Brent remarked.
~~~

"True." Carter scratched his head, unconvinced.

"You could just ask her," Brent said with another laugh. "I have nothing useful to offer. I haven't spoken to a woman in months. I couldn't begin to tell you what goes on in their heads."

Carter finally found a smile. "You're probably right. Getting myself all worked up about it isn't going to do anyone any good. I'll go into the village tomorrow and wire Fred for some information about her. I'd like to know where he found her at the very least. I should have done that from the beginning. When I wired him with my requirements and trusted him to fulfill them, I didn't give thought to how very foolish I was to not ask him any questions when he wired back that everything was said and done. I was just relieved that I wasn't going to have to return to Boston to make the arrangements myself."

Brent kept steadily brushing his horse but pondered the situation. "I still don't understand why you were so averse to going there and finding her yourself."

"I don't plan on ever going back to that dreadful place for the rest of my days, if I can help it."

"But I'm thinking arranging for a wife is a serious thing. Why did you want one from Boston if you're so firm and determined not to go there? Don't you think she might want to visit some time?"

"No, we need to keep my wife satisfied here. There's nothing for us in Boston." Carter could hear the determination in his voice and realized he didn't sound completely reasonable, but he couldn't bring himself to care.

"Not even your family?"

Carter laughed but it sounded grim. "My family is most of the reason I don't want to go back there. While I miss my brother, there's no love lost between me and my father. And his friends. They would just make my life miserable. Besides after living out here where life is so large, I shudder at the thought of spending any time in a city."

"But why did you want a wife from there if you think the place is so bad?"

"I figured she'd understand where I come from if she comes from there, too." Now he sounded sulky. Carter was becoming fed up with himself.

"Do you still think that now that you've met her?" Brent was curious.

Carter shrugged. "Too soon to tell, I suppose."

"She sure is pretty, though," Brent commented. "Not that I got that good of a stare at her, since you rushed her into the house so fast."

Carter could feel color rising in his cheeks and tried to ignore his embarrassment. "You and the other men aren't to be looking at my wife."

Brent stared at his boss with his eyebrows reaching into his floppy hair. "Really?" he asked, his tone dry and sarcastic. "How are we supposed to accomplish that?"

"Just don't look at her," Carter insisted.

"Do you plan on keeping her locked up in the house?" Brent was now sounding incredulous.

Carter thought about striking the man who was his right hand on the land as well as his friend. "Of course not."

"Then how do you expect us not to look at her?" Brent was obviously becoming frustrated. "If she needs a horse saddled or is offering us a meal, we're gonna have to look at her, at least a little bit."

Carter stared at the other man for a minute before finally starting to chuckle. "I think I'm losing my mind." He scratched his head, staring off toward the hayloft. Bringing his gaze back to his friend he finally admitted, "I didn't expect her to be so pretty."

"You were expecting an ugly woman?"

Carter shrugged.

"Did you want an ugly woman?" Brent's gentle emphasis on "want" and his gentled tone made Carter laugh again.

"Not particularly, but I was expecting one. I just can't figure out why she would agree to this arrangement. I expected someone who was desperate. She doesn't look like she'd be at all desperate for a husband. Surely she could have her pick."

"Now I begin to understand your confusion." Brent shrugged. "Like I said, you'll have to talk to her about it. I can't help you with this. What I can tell you is the crew is ready to ride out and collect the herd from the back lot whenever you give the word."

"Good. I don't want to go tomorrow, though, since she just got here. She'd probably be nervous if I leave her completely on her own so soon. Let's set everyone to checking fences tomorrow. We'll ride out the next day."

Brent's expression was skeptical. "Do you really think she'll be ready to be left alone by the next day?"

Carter shrugged again. "Don't see why not."

Brent just shook his head and grinned as he turned away to put his tools away. The horse he had been working on was finished and ready to settle in for the night.

"Have a great night, Boss," he added as he left the barn, leaving Carter behind, still not finished with his tasks even though he was usually the fastest one done with the chores.

Shaking his head, Carter tried to get his mind back on the matters at hand and away from wondering what his new wife was up to in his new house.

Chapter Six

Ella walked around the stark room. It certainly was spacious. Of course, space was one thing that wasn't lacking out here in the rugged West. But there was nothing comfortable or cozy about the cavernous chamber. She gazed around again. Maybe it was because it was all so new. Perhaps with time it would mellow and grow cozy. Her gaze sharpened. Perhaps some curtains would help. Having so many windows was a luxury but with them all just there, open and bright, it didn't really present itself as being very homey.

Ella brightened. She knew how to make curtains. Of course, she didn't have any fabric. But surely they would have some if there was a mercantile in the village nearby. Surely it couldn't be called a village if there wasn't a mercantile. Or if they ever went back to the Town where the train station was, she had seen at least two or three shops that would likely have fabric. She would have to speak to Mr. McLain about it. Actually, she suddenly recalled that he had mentioned there was a mercantile, when he had mentioned his distaste toward going to the Town. He had seemed quite convinced that it was sufficiently stocked. She would trust that they would have a fabric supply.

She sighed. Ella should've asked him what he wanted to be called when he had been asking her. Imagine him wanting to call her Mrs. McLain. She would never answer him if he did that. It would certainly take some getting used to, that was for sure.

Looking around the room again, Ella realized that it really did have a great deal of potential. A few homey touches here and there and it would be quite lovely. She could host all sorts of entertainments in a room this big. She couldn't help but laugh over that thought. Who would she entertain out her in the middle of the great beyond? But it cheered her anyway. At least she wasn't to live in a hovel.

Ella peaked out one of the windows and saw the house he said he used to live in. Even it wouldn't have been so bad. She had tried not to envision anything about her new home while she was riding out here on the train, but she couldn't help imagining what it might be like. Unfortunately her imagination had conjured up worse and worse images the closer she got to her destination. So while she couldn't say she loved her new home, it was by far better than what she had been dreading as a possibility. And really, with a few feminine touches, the new house could actually feel like a home rather easily.

Continuing her investigations, Ella felt bad that she wasn't enraptured with the house. It was obvious that a lot of work had gone into its construction. Clearly her new husband was a hard worker. And he had included many practical touches, like hooks on the wall beside every door so that things could be kept tidy. She would appreciate that when it came time to clean. She couldn't help grinning. She was going to be responsible for cleaning an entire house. Her mother would be aghast. But if her parents hadn't wanted her to end up in this situation, they should have been more careful with their own actions, she thought with a mental flounce.

And since they hadn't been careful, they should be relieved that she was ending up in a reasonably decent environment. Her husband seemed like a gentleman, even if he appeared to be somewhat moody. And even though she was far from shopping and society, if you asked her, that was a blessing, not a curse. She had experienced more than enough of society's views, and she could do without it for the time being at the very least. Ella was looking forward to getting to know her own company for a while.

Approaching the stairs, Ella wondered if she should venture upstairs. She felt as though she were prying or being nosy. But he had said to make herself feel at home. Surely if she felt at home she would know every single corner of the house. She was standing with one foot on the bottom step, still debating with herself about going up to see what was surely bedrooms, when Carter burst through the front door.

When he saw her standing there, hesitating, his eyebrows rose.

"Have you been upstairs yet?"

"No," she admitted. "I felt as though I was invading your privacy."

He laughed. "I suppose it's your privacy now, too. You'll have to take one of the bedrooms upstairs, too. Unless you would prefer I move out to the barn for the time being."

Ella bit her lip. A part of her wanted to agree wholeheartedly with his suggestion, but since they were legally wed and this was the man's home, surely it would be unseemly to ask him to sleep with the cattle. She supposed she could offer to do so. She brought herself to task, mentally at least.

"Don't be silly, we can manage quite well if there are separate bed chambers here."

"Very well, then let's go up and you can pick which room you'd like to use for the next three months."

Ella bit her lip again at the reminder that her reprieve was temporary. Surely by the end of the three months she would know her husband better and feel more comfortable with actually being married to him. Or at least she most wholeheartedly believed so. She hoped her sigh wasn't audible as she preceded him up the stairs.

Her concerns were pushed from her mind when she reached the top of the stairs and looked about. While it was still rather stark from a lack of any warming touches, there was a great deal of potential to be seen. There were four rooms down a short hallway, each with their own doors. And it would appear that each room also had its own window, some rooms appeared to even have two windows in them. The luxury of it was rather decadent. Ella took a deep breath in anticipation of how fresh the air was sure to be.

"Either you have a great deal of money or there is no window tax out this way," she remarked.

Carter chuckled from behind her. "Not much taxes of any sort hereabouts," was all he offered in the way of information, though. Ella chose not to pry even though she wanted to press for more information. Was he not afraid that such a tax would arrive? Even her parents, who had been quite well to do, had chosen to have a couple of their windows bricked up to reduce their taxation.

He interrupted the flow of her thoughts by stepping past her.

"I've been using this room, as it's the biggest, but you can have it for now, if you'd like."

"Oh no, I wouldn't want to put you out of your chamber."

"I don't have much stuff and surely, as a woman, you'll have more than I ever will."

Ella's face heated. She didn't really have many things either. "I don't have much with me either. I can manage quite nicely in one of the other rooms." She peeked her head into one. "In fact, this looks like it will do just fine."

"The morning sun comes in on this side. It'll wake you up for sure."

"That's probably a good thing, isn't it? Won't we need to be up with the sun? Without something to wake me, I doubt I'll do so on my own."

Carter chuckled again. Ella couldn't be sure if he was mocking her spoiled background or pleased that she was willing to adjust. She didn't think Fred had told him much about her, so he probably didn't know about her spoiled background. As a man, her gowns probably didn't tell him as much as they would tell a woman. She felt a little lighter at the thought. He was probably pleased with her. That was a comforting thought even if it wasn't necessarily true. She really ought to try to communicate with him. Maybe when she felt a little more settled.

Now that was circular reasoning at its best, she mocked herself. She would communicate with him when she felt more comfortable with him. But how was she to feel more comfortable with him without communication? It was a conundrum she wasn't going to be able to solve at that moment.

Her new husband was rubbing his hands together and looking at her expectantly. "I'm feeling quite hungry after the long drive. What do you suppose we should have for lunch?"

Ella stared at the man, wondering if he was again mocking her. He was returning her regard, not revealing his thoughts, his face impassive. She blinked first and offered him as bright a smile as she could muster.

"I have yet to examine the larder, I'm afraid. Shall we retire to the kitchen to see what we can manage on short notice?"

She was gratified to see that he was surprised she had not run screaming from the room at his words. *What did he think I was going to do, refuse to cook for him?* While she didn't have much experience, Sybil's staff had been as thorough as possible in her brief lessons.

When they reached the kitchen, Ella blessed the Boston cook for her foresight in realizing she would need some easy, simple recipes. At first, when Ella had approached the woman asking to be taught, Ella had visions of roast duck dripping in orange sauce and cheese soufflé with lobster bisque, but Cook had declared the need to keep it simple. She didn't have time to learn fancy fixin's, and there would be little need out in the frontier for such things, anyway. They were a little far from the harbor for lobster, that was for sure.

The larder was better equipped than the cook had feared, and Ella was relieved to recognize some of the items. But she was tired and hungry herself. She couldn't be bothered to go to too great an effort. Lifting the latch she had spied in the floor, she was relieved to see a cold cellar beneath the floor.

"Would eggs and toast, and perhaps some fried ham, suffice? I'm afraid at this point I'm too tired to attempt anything else."

Mr. McLain, who had been watching her carefully without comment, grinned. "That would hit the spot just fine, thank you. Perhaps a cup of tea or coffee wouldn't go down hard, either."

Ella was dismayed. Coffee was one of the things she had trouble mastering. She could never get the measurement just right. She hadn't realized she had such finicky tastes, nor how perfectly her former staff had brewed the beverage. Whenever she made it, she found it was either too weak or too strong.

"Would tea be satisfactory to you? I'm not so good at making coffee."

"I'm decent at it. If you'd like a cup, I could make it."

She tried to hide her surprise at his offer. At least the man didn't intend to simply stand by and watch her. While he had offered his assistance on the drive to his property, she hadn't really expected him to follow through. She smiled her appreciation. "I would love a cup, thank you."

They bustled around, working in surprising harmony although the room didn't feel nearly as spacious as she had first thought with the both of them in it. She was distractedly aware of the large, handsome man as she moved around the room, trying to avoid brushing against him as they exchanged places. It was beginning to almost feel like a dance. Like a cotillion where the partners kept changing. She suppressed a smile at the thought. There would be no more debutante dances for her.

The room began to fill with the heady aromas of the frying foods, and Ella's cheeks heated as her stomach grumbled audibly.

"I thought you ate enough at breakfast to no longer be starving," McLain remarked.

Ella had nothing to say in response, keeping her head bowed in a vain attempt to hide her burning face.

"It would seem your hunger extended beyond just a missed breakfast." She could feel his gaze burning into the back of her head as she continued busily at the stove, still without an answer.

"Did they run out of supplies on the train?" he persisted in questioning her.

"I couldn't really say."

"Why not? Why did you allow yourself to go hungry? Seems mighty foolish if you ask me, and you don't really strike me as a fool."

Ella was momentarily gratified by his observation. But it wasn't sufficient to distract her from her concerns. She didn't really want to reveal the depths of her desperation. Although why that was, she couldn't have really explained. Pride, no doubt.

"Are you trying to keep secrets from me, Mrs. McLain?"

Her eyes finally flew to his face. Despite his pleasant tone, his face revealed that he was becoming angry at her silence.

"I had no money," she told him grudgingly. "Must you force me to spell it out? Did you expect you were marrying an heiress?" She was going on the defensive.

"Of course not, but why didn't you ask Fred to lend you some funds? I would've arranged to reimburse him."

"I wasn't to know that, though, was I? We've never met before today."

"I'm surprised Fred didn't think of it. Did he not know your circumstances?"

Ella shrugged. "It really doesn't matter at this point, does it? I'm here now and from the looks of it, I needn't go hungry again. I thank you for the provisions."

"I'm not looking for your gratitude, Ella, I'm looking for information."

"What information do you want?"

"All of it," he declared in frustration.

Her face must've revealed her confusion because he finally elaborated while his face remained inscrutable.

"I want to know why you accepted my proposal through Fred. Were you just looking for an adventure out West and thought this was the best way to accomplish it? Aside from your hunger, nothing about you declares desperation, so I'm trying to understand why you agreed to this."

Once again, Ella went on the defensive. "Were you looking for a desperate wife? What's wrong with you that you needed to take advantage of a woman's desperation? Why couldn't you find a wife on your own without getting Fred to find some poor female who has fallen on hard times and has nowhere else to turn?"

She might have gone too far with her questions as Carter's face reddened. She feared she had angered him, so she was shocked when he burst into laughter.

"I can see your point. Clearly I hadn't thought the matter all the way through when I asked Fred to find me a wife. It was only after you were already on your way that I questioned what manner of woman would agree to such an arrangement. To be honest, it was me who was desperate. I desperately did not want to return to Boston, but for some inexplicable reason, I wanted my wife to be from there, as though that would somehow give us common roots."

Ella nodded. "I can see the sense in that. Common roots could lead to common values."

Carter nodded too, but then shook his head. "But I've been out here so long, I've probably been molded in a different way than your experiences have molded you."

Ella shrugged. "That would be true even if we were both born, raised, and stayed in the same area. You being a man would give you a different perspective and set of experiences than I would have."

Carter nodded, deep in thought, as though he were struck by her words. But then his gaze flew to her, and his eyes narrowed. "You've gone and turned the subject, and I still know nothing about you."

Ella laughed, although she could hear for herself that it sounded forced. "I'm sorry, I just went with the flow of the conversation."

"You're still doing it." Carter blew out a frustrated breath. "Tell me about your family."

"I am an orphan, I'm afraid to say. I was an only child. My parents doted on me. But they died very suddenly six months ago."

"Oh, I'm sorry for your loss. You've taken on a great deal of changes, then, this year. Was that wise?"

Ella smiled, hoping it didn't look like the grimace it felt to be, and shrugged. It wasn't as though she were given a great deal of choice in the matter.

"My parents' death forced change on me. This arrangement seemed to be the best of my options. And I truly was happy to leave Boston behind. I didn't make this decision lightly, or on a whim, if that is what concerns you. I took advisement from close friends, and we all agreed this had the potential of providing me with a much better future than staying in Boston held for me."

"And now that you've arrived, do you still feel the same way?"

Ella couldn't tell if he was just curious or actually looking for reassurance. She dismissed the ludicrous idea. The handsome, rugged man certainly didn't lack for confidence. It's not as though he needed any sort of comfort from her.

"I have yet to see anything to greatly change my mind on the matter," she said with a smile. It was the truth. While she had been disconcerted by how handsome the man was, everything that she had seen so far about him was reassuring rather than off putting. And while the house was in desperate need of a few feminine touches to make it feel like a home, they were not things she could take umbrage with. All in all, she had feared going into the unknown situation and had dreaded the potential hazards. So far, she hadn't seen anything to cause her alarm, but to the contrary, she was feeling reassured by everything she had seen thus far.

Chapter Seven

Carter was entertained as he watched emotions flit across his wife's face. He was coming to realize that she was the furthest thing from a chatterbox he had ever met in the female form. Coming from Boston, he had expected her to be hard to silence rather than hard to initiate conversation with. But from what he could tell so far, it didn't really seem like a deliberate attempt to keep something from him specifically, but rather a deep seated attempt to keep to herself, isolated and independent. He would have to try a little harder.

But knowing she was an orphan explained a few things. Perhaps she didn't have any means of support after the death of her father, although she had mentioned seeking advice from some trusted friends. After they ate, he would set off to the village to send his wire to Fred. He berated himself for not thinking of it earlier. He could have had the information before she even arrived.

"How do you like your eggs?"

"Pardon?"

"Do you like the yellow part to be runny or not?"

Carter blinked at her. He'd never thought of it before. He always just cooked them. They turned out how they turned out.

"Uh, can it be a little of both?" He grinned thinking he had stumped her, but she simply nodded.

When she placed the plate in front of him he was surprised to see how well prepared everything seemed. Even the toast was the perfect light brown that he personally loved but found hard to achieve. For someone who claimed not to have much cooking knowledge, she had done an excellent job. His suspicions began to resurface.

"I have chores to do this evening, before dark. You'll have plenty to keep you occupied, won't you?"

He didn't understand the blank expression on her face that immediately followed his question, but she promptly nodded and answered, "Of course," so he didn't think too much about it.

After swallowing back his last bite of the delicious meal, along with his last sip of the coffee, he got to his feet and prepared to depart.

"That was much better than I had expected, thank you."

She appeared amused by his words but accepted them with a nod and a smile. Carter realized his compliment was rather backhanded and felt chagrined.

"I meant you no insult, ma'am. I just thought from you saying you weren't very experienced that it would be a mite worse than it was."

Her amusement deepened. "I'm glad it turned out. I'll be practising on you over the next while."

Carter could feel color rising in his cheeks. He was just making it worse. He jammed his hat on his head and left without saying anything else. He didn't want to tell her where he was going, and trying to say anything else was just making him feel increasingly awkward.

Brent raised his eyebrows when he saw Carter leading his horse out of its stall. "You leaving your bride behind so soon?"

"Something I need to do in the village."

Brent grinned. "She have you jumping to her demands already?"

"Nope." Carter wasn't going to start explaining himself at this moment, even if he could've explained it. He could barely understand his motivations himself.

He was glad his horse knew the way because most of Carter's mind was occupied with trying to figure out how to word his questions so as to not provide too much gossip for the village but to get as much information as possible from Fred.

Package arrived

Need more information

Write if too private for wire

It wasn't perfect, but it would get the point across, he was sure. Carter sighed. He hoped so anyway. It had been years since he'd seen Fred in person. They had been boyhood friends, growing up in the same Boston neighborhood and even being sent to the same boarding school when they were in their early teens. They had gone to different universities but had remained friends, visiting each other's campus and spending time with each other's families. He trusted Fred, despite the fact that they had gone in drastically different directions with their lives since reaching adulthood.

Fred should've known to provide the needed information without him needing to ask, Carter thought, starting to feel a little peevish as he rode back toward his house. But then his suspicions kicked in again. Maybe he had sent a message through his wife and she had not been forthcoming with it. He resolved to ask her as soon as he returned home.

Riding into the yard, Carter felt his usual pride puff up his chest as he observed all that was his. He wasn't trying to be egotistical on the matter, but considered he deserved to be proud of what he had accomplished from more than a decade of hard, laborious work. And now he had a wife to share it with. He grinned. A beautiful wife. But a wife he couldn't trust. This brought him back down to earth quickly and he jumped down from his horse and led it into the barn to be brushed and stabled.

Making quick work of his chores and after checking with Brent and the other men, Carter was able to make his way into the house just as the sun made its final splash of light as it descended behind the trees.

The house was filled with the most delicious scent it had ever contained in its short life. Carter couldn't place his finger on what exactly he was smelling but he took deep, appreciative sniffs as he unlaced his boots.

"Hello?" he called out, not seeing his wife and not wanting to startle her by appearing unexpectedly.

She poked her head out from the larder. He hadn't noticed that the door there was ajar.

"Hello," she answered softly. "Are you finished with your chores for the day?"

"I am," he said without going into detail about where he'd been.

"Are you nearly ready to eat? I should have asked you what time you normally have your evening meal. We had our lunch so late, I wasn't sure if you would want a big meal or not. So I made a little bit of everything, I'm afraid."

She was babbling, much to Carter's surprise. It seemed like the most words she had strung together in his presence since her arrival. He couldn't restrain his grin but tried not to tease her.

"I'm not ravenous, but I could definitely eat. This is a perfect time, most days. I like to take advantage of the light and get as much done out of doors as possible. And if I'm near home, I prefer the bigger meal of the day to be around noon, so it's perfect if you have a lighter meal prepared now."

He was startled to see how relieved she seemed by his words. She seemed to be a nervous little thing. Carter wondered about it. What would make a beautiful, articulate woman so insecure? He supposed her sudden changes of circumstances wouldn't contribute to a sense of security.

He tried to be offhanded as he asked her, "Did Fred by any chance send me any messages with you?"

Her confusion appeared to be genuine as she replied. "No, were you expecting him to?"

Carter shrugged. "Not really, I was just wondering. I haven't heard from him in ages."

Her confusion did not lighten. "Did you know him prior to your dealings in connection with your search for a wife?"

Carter grinned again. "We grew up around each other. My mother worked in his house before my father struck it rich. She died working too hard. But we became friends and went to school together. Did he not tell you anything?"

She shook her head. "Apparently not."

"And you didn't ask?"

She shook her head again. "Apparently not the right questions, anyway."

"What did you ask him?" By now he had washed his hands and wiped his face on a towel and had taken his seat at the table, waiting patiently as she served up what looked to be a delicious meal.

Now she looked embarrassed. "I asked him for a description of you so I would be able to find you when I arrived."

Carter chuckled. Her tone lead him to believe the description had been less than accurate. "How did he describe me?"

"He said you were tall with brown hair," she said, sounding even more disgruntled.

"Well that's true," he said, wondering what the problem could possibly be. "I was afraid you were going to say he had told you something ridiculous like that I have orange hair and stand five feet tall."

His wife looked confused by his words. "Why would you have thought that?"

"It was just the sort of sense of humor he had back when we were boys." He waved away any comment she might have made and hurried on with another question. "I must ask, then, if his description wasn't so bad, why did you sound as though it was wrong."

He found the huffy expression on her face amusing but he tried to stifle it, instinctively realising she would not appreciate thinking he was laughing at her.

"It may have been accurate on the surface. Yes, you are tall, and yes, your hair is brown, but it also described at least half of the men in the town we were in!"

Carter chuckled. "I can see what you mean when you put it like that. Well how would you have described me, if you were Fred, so that you could have distinguished me from all the others?"

He was intrigued by the bright red color that splashed across her cheekbones at his question. Even more amusing was her stuttering attempt to answer him.

"Oh, well, I wouldn't possibly know how Fred would have described you, as I'm beginning to realize that perhaps men look at these things a bit differently. But if I was the one arranging for you to meet up with an acquaintance of mine, I would be sure to tell you a distinguishing feature or an item of clothing that would mark you as different."

"Well, what would have set me apart from everyone else?" He wasn't sure why he persisted except that her obvious reluctance increased his curiosity. "I rather think I was dressed like everyone else besides being tall and brown haired."

She was silent for much longer than he would have thought necessary to answer what ought to be a simple question. When she finally spoke, even her neck was turning red. He started to be concerned for her health.

"You had the bluest eyes there. The bluest I've ever seen. That would have been a useful piece of information."

Carter grunted, slightly taken aback by her reply. "Why was that so hard to say? I don't really examine myself that carefully, but I dare say you're right about my eyes. I used to get teased something fierce about them when I was growing up."

She tried to squirm away from answering his questions but he admired her fidelity when she squared her shoulders, looked him in the eye and answered him. It was apparent her truthfulness cost her a measure of comfort.

"No one would tease you about them now, I dare say. You are the most handsome man I've ever seen. That's how I would have described you to someone meeting you for the first time." The laugh she uttered displayed all her obvious nervousness.

"But it's probably not what men would say, though, is it?"

Carter tried not to let her words go straight to his ego, but it was a difficult thing. He could feel his chest expanding with her words. "You think I'm handsome?"

Her face must hurt, he thought, with how red it's burning. She was obviously finished with difficult truths. She brushed her hands down her skirts and moved around the room restlessly. She didn't answer his question.

"Might I ask, what should I know about the coming days? What do you expect of me? Am I to cook for your men? Or just you and me? And are there any other chores you expect me to do, besides looking after the house and food?"

Carter blinked. He hadn't been prepared for her sudden turn of topic. "How about we ease into things as we go along?"

He didn't really like the skeptical expression on her face. Her lips compressed as though she were holding back her words. He wished she would just tell him what was on her mind. Carter sighed. He supposed if he didn't trust her, it wasn't likely that she could be expected to trust him.

It wasn't long before they retired for the night. Carter doubted he would be able to sleep but he needed to rest at the very least. There was much that needed to be done the next day and he needed as many of his faculties about him as he could manage.

He was consumed with pondering about the woman across the hallway. Carter certainly hoped

Fred would get back to him as quickly as possible, but he didn't think he could go to the village every day without raising suspicions in his wife. Not that she seemed to be an overly nosy female. Maybe he could. Because he certainly couldn't settle until he had more information.

Chapter Eight

Ella stared into the darkness. Or rather into the gloom. It wasn't nearly as dark as she was used to at night here with the uncovered windows. The moon was nearly full and cast bright light into the room, creating startling shadows. She closed her eyes to block out the eerie sights. With all the thoughts whirling through her head, she was already going to have a difficult enough time getting to sleep; she didn't need to compound the problem by scaring herself out of her wits with gazing about at creepy shadows.

With a sigh, Ella flopped onto her other side, bunching her pillow under her ear, trying to find a comfortable position. She ought to be sleeping like a baby since the bed was far more comfortable than she had expected, and she hadn't had a decent night's sleep in days, but the oblivion of slumber evaded her.

Squeezing her eyes shut, Ella tried counting, focusing her thoughts on steadying her breathing, trying not to think about her husband's high, strong cheekbones, clear, blue eyes, and the tuft of dark hair that kept tumbling over his eyebrow, tempting her fingers to reach up and push it out of his line of sight. And his voice! Whenever he spoke it caused shivers to shimmy up her spine and gooseflesh to break out on her arms. She was being ridiculous. Ella attempted to rein in her thoughts once more, resuming her counting and deep breathing.

Thankfully, the long day and her exhaustion finally caught up to her and she was pulled under into a deep, dreamless sleep.

The bright sunlight streaming through her uncovered window woke Ella early the next morning. She stretched and yawned, of two minds about facing the new day. She was anxious to get on with starting her new life, but she was apprehensive about facing her new husband, uncertain of his expectations. Never one to dawdle, Ella pulled herself from the comfortable bed and got on with the day.

After a mostly silent meal of fried eggs and what turned out to be the last of the bread, Ella hoped she was doing it right as she started the bread making process before she went out to wander around the yard. Thankfully, it was one of the lessons Sybil's cook had covered, but Ella wasn't feeling terribly confident in her ability to successfully replicate the light and airy bread Cook had produced.

"Good day, ma'am."

Ella almost turned to see who the man was addressing but realized it was her just before embarrassing herself.

"Good morning," she replied, wondering who the slightly scruffy young man was.

"I'm Brent, the foreman of this spread."

Ella stuck her hand out to shake. "Nice to meet you, Brent. I'm Ella." She didn't elaborate on her name. It would probably be disrespectful toward her husband if she used her maiden name, but she wasn't yet comfortable with the thought of identifying herself as a McLain. She suddenly recalled he had told her he didn't want the men to be overly familiar with her, but it was too late now.

Her dilemma must've been displayed on her face because the foreman grinned but he didn't say anything, merely lifting his hat slightly and acknowledging her words with another polite, "ma'am." Ella could feel her color rising. She didn't feel like a ma'am but she supposed she was and would have to accept it. She couldn't be expecting anyone to call her miss, and she supposed she was just as glad to leave her maiden name behind. She had adored her parents, but now their name only brought her trouble.

"Is there anything I can do for you, ma'am?"

The man's words interrupted her troubled thoughts, for which Ella was grateful. She shrugged. "Not that I know of, but thank you. I was just going to take a look around before I get on with my chores. It seems to be a beautiful day."

"That it is, ma'am."

Ella was becoming a little frustrated with his continued polite emphasis on her married status. Was he trying to remind her that she was a married woman? She wasn't likely to forget. She could feel her smile tighten but tried to maintain a grip on her temper. With nothing more to say to the man, she stepped away, heading toward the first barn she could see.

"Ma'am, step carefully. We haven't cleaned up the yard here yet, and many animals have passed through."

Ella glanced down and realized he had prevented her from stepping into a smelly mess. Feeling heat climb her cheeks, Ella was torn between gratitude that he had helped her and embarrassment that she had required the reminder. While she was city bred, the problem was a universal one if you were ever crossing a street. She waved in acknowledgment of his words and continued carefully on toward the barn.

It was cooler and darker inside the large, wooden structure. Ella took a deep, appreciative breath. This space was clearly kept cleaner than the yard. All she could smell was fresh hay. The barn was nearly empty. Ella wondered why the foreman was still around if everyone else had left to work elsewhere on the property.

"Are you certain I can't help you with anything?"

Ella nearly squeaked as she jumped and whirled toward the voice. She hadn't heard Brent follow her into the barn.

"Why are you following me?" She squinted her eyes at him, full of suspicion.

"I was just trying to watch out for you, ma'am. It's rather apparent you aren't from around here. Wouldn't want you to hurt yourself on your first day."

Cheeks burning, Ella tried to be grateful but all she felt was resentment. She didn't need a minder. He saved her from needing to respond by turning the subject.

"Were you by any chance looking for the horses? Or maybe the lambs?"

Ella didn't want to admit that she hadn't a clue what animals there might be on the farm, except that she had been expecting to see at least a few cows, so she merely nodded, making the man laugh.

"We had a surprise batch of lambs born just a couple days ago. The rest of the ewes gave birth weeks ago and those babies are getting pretty big by now, but come through here to the next barn and you'll be able to see the new babies."

Ella was delighted. She tried to appear unaffected, but she couldn't wait to see the lambs now that he had told her about them. She lifted her skirt and hurried to keep up with his long strides.

The babies were delightful. Ella was well aware that babies of any species were appealing, but there was just something about the lambs that was drawing her in. She didn't even mind when they nibbled on her hem and butted against her legs.

"Your pretty dress is going to get grubby if you don't have a care, ma'am."

She hadn't realized he was still there. It startled her, but she appreciated his obvious concern for her wellbeing. But she wasn't going to be gainsaid from her fun.

"That's quite all right. It can be washed. These babies are just so darling, I cannot be bothered to prevent them from rubbing on me."

"Have you never seen lambs before, ma'am?"

Ella grinned. His constant calling of her ma'am had been grating on her nerves, but now it was starting to amuse her. She tried to recall his question.

"No, I can't say that I ever have. At least not in real life. Maybe in a painting. But no painting could ever capture how very captivating they are. And their plaintive bleating. I shouldn't find it so amusing, I suppose, but I just want to cuddle them all."

The foreman laughed along with her. "I never really thought about how someone unused to them might see them. I'm glad you like them."

Ella looked up with a sigh. "I suppose I ought to return to the house and get on with preparing a meal. From the looks of the sun, noon is fast approaching."

Brent scratched his head. The look he cast her was full of skepticism. "I think you have a bit more time to spare. Would you like me to show you a little bit more of the property before you head in?"

Ella hadn't been too full of enthusiasm for the tasks that awaited her inside, so she quickly accepted.

It was all new to her and it struck her that her husband's property must be vast indeed as the foreman showed her around.

"Do the animals out in the fields not have a shelter? Why would they be allowed to roam so far?"

"There's no need for them to live in a barn as they aren't dairy cows. They have thick coats that protect them through the winter months. We do like to have them closer so we can check on them, though, whenever there's a particularly cold spell, but for the most part, they huddle together and manage quite well."

"But why allow them to get so far away in the first place?"

Brent shrugged. "They like to roam. And your husband has enough property that it isn't an issue. When they spread out over the land, it leaves enough grazing for all of them."

"Doesn't it leave them susceptible to predators if they're spread all over the place?"

"It can. But your husband has some men that also roam around, keeping an eye on the herds and providing protection when necessary."

Ella shivered. "What kind of predators might be around?"

Brent shrugged. "Bears, coyotes, wolves, mountain lions."

Ella could feel her eyes growing wider and wider with each animal he listed. Brent chuckled at her expression.

"Not all at once, and most of them are rarely seen in these parts. But we have lost a few animals in the time I've been here. You just asked what might be around. Those might be."

Ella looked around at the tranquil scene before her and gulped. She was just beginning to think she needed to return to the house where there was no chance of encountering a wild animal when her husband strode toward them.

"You two look deep in discussion. I hope I'm not disturbing you."

He sounded angry, and Ella's stomach clenched.

"I'm sorry. I let the time get away on me. I meant to have your meal ready for you when you arrived. If you'll excuse me, I'll get to that right away."

Without waiting for a reply from either man, she lifted her skirts and hurried to the house, leaving a momentary silence in her wake.

Chapter Nine

"What's gotten into you?" Brent asked. Carter could feel heat filling his face. He tried to ignore his embarrassment.

"I didn't think I had to tell you to stay away from my wife. I expected to need to warn the other men, but not you."

"So, you expected me to ignore her when she came outside wanting to investigate your property? I thought I was doing you a service to keep her from harm."

Carter could see the other man becoming belligerent in his indignation over Carter's implication.

"I was surprised to see the two of you looking so deep in conversation."

Brent shrugged. "She had a few questions about your spread. I answered them."

"What kind of questions?"

Brent sighed. "I don't know, questions. She obviously doesn't know much about animals and such. She wanted to know why the cattle roam and would they be all right on their own."

"Why'd she ask you that?"

"Probably because I was here. Maybe you shoulda been. Where were you off to when you could have been here answering your new wife's questions?"

Carter again fought the rise of heat in his cheeks, refusing to acknowledge the truth of his friend's words. He had ridden into the village hoping there had been word from Fred, but there were no messages awaiting him. If Fred chose to write, it could be a week or more before he heard anything. Carter had been hoping to receive a telegram, but perhaps whatever Fred might have to tell him was too private. Carter would have to ride into the village daily until he got the information he sought. But he didn't want to share that information with his foreman, even though he would trust him with his life. He wouldn't have been able to explain why, if he had been asked.

"Never mind about where I was. Get back to your work."

Brent raised his eyebrows at his boss' unusually curt manner but didn't respond other than to lift his hat sardonically and turn on his heel. Carter watched him walk away and wished he could call back his words. Brent was his friend besides his employee. And he would trust him with everything he had. Except his wife. She was too beautiful. And he didn't trust her either.

That reminder sent him heading toward the house. He needed to keep his eyes on her. Who knew what sort of mischief she could get up to in his house. He ignored Brent's chuckle coming from behind him. It wouldn't do to acknowledge the man's disrespect. He didn't care if they were friends. He was the boss and his word was final.

His long strides ate up the distance and within seconds he was standing on the porch. He felt a moment's hesitation before he barged into the house. She was in the kitchen, stirring something fragrant on the stove. His mouth watered and he wasn't sure if it was the woman or the food that drew his attention more. He was a little disgusted with himself. How could he be so attracted to a woman he wasn't sure he could trust?

"I'm almost finished," she called over her shoulder. "I'm sorry I wasn't ready when you were. I got caught up with admiring the lambs."

The smile she cast at him appeared even more nervous than usual. His suspicious mind ratcheted up another notch. He needed to get to the bottom of his suspicions of her. But then he noticed she was chewing on her lip, and it dawned on him that she was genuinely nervous, that she was truly concerned that she hadn't had his meal ready right at the stroke of noon.

"Don't worry about it," he was surprised to hear himself saying. "Nothing needs to be timed down to the very second. I'm just relieved that I don't have to cook for myself anymore."

She blushed at his words, as though pleased by them. Carter felt his brows furrowing. He didn't know what to make of this woman. Once again, he hoped Fred sent him some information soon.

Carter determined to return to the village first thing the next day.

Ella placed the steaming bowl in front of him filled with what looked like a thick stew. Then she placed a plate piled high with bread on the table.

"Did you just bake this today?" He could see it was still warm.

"Yes, we finished off all the bread you had this morning."

"How did you find the time?"

Her face scrunched up in confusion. "I don't understand your question."

"You were outside wandering around," he pointed out. "How did you have time to make bread?"

She laughed. "I put it in the oven before I went outside. As luck would have it, your arrival made me come in before I burnt it. So thank you for that. I would have felt dreadful if I had burnt my first batch of bread."

"What do you mean by your first batch? You mean in your new kitchen?"

Now she truly looked uncomfortable. Her eyes flitted around the room, as though she were trying to avoid his gaze.

"Yes," she finally answered him, which was not at all informative. He let out a sigh. She was no closer to trusting him than he was to her.

Carter shovelled the stew into his mouth. It was delicious, but now he could barely taste it. All he wanted to do was get out of the house. He hoped there was plenty of hard manual labor to keep him occupied that afternoon. If there weren't enough chores, he would split wood. He needed to work off his frustration while he waited for any sort of explanation.

~~~

Several hours later, he returned to the yard to find his wife deep in conversation with Brent once more. Carter realized the sensation swelling in his chest was jealousy, but there wasn't much he could do about it. He ought to tell her to stay inside. He certainly shouldn't punch his foreman in the face like he wished to, so Carter tried to rein in his temper.

It didn't improve his mood to realize that his arrival put a quick end to their conversation. Ella took one look at him and started toward the house with a backward wave to Brent. Carter watched her walk away while he sat astride his large horse.

"I thought I was fairly clear on my feelings about you visiting with my wife."

"You certainly were," was Brent's cheerful reply.

Carter thought he might grind his teeth into dust as he clenched them in an effort to keep his emotions in check. "And yet here you are."

"Yes, here I am. Look, McLain, if you don't want me talking to your wife, you ought to tell her about it. I have no intention of being rude to the poor woman. She just wants to learn about your property and have someone to talk to. It's far from a social hub around here."

"She can talk to me if she wants someone to talk to." Carter could hear the temper in his own ears but he tried to regain control of his emotions.
~~~

Brent lifted a sardonic eyebrow. "Perhaps you ought to tell her that, McLain. It's not as though you've been around for her to talk to even if she wanted to. She wanted to spend more time with the lambs. Apparently you told her she could have a pet. She was wondering if a lamb might be a good pet. You'll be happy, I'm sure, to know that I was able to convince her that while they would probably appreciate her visits, they wouldn't enjoy living in your house."

Carter growled, without intelligent words. He couldn't deny what Brent was saying. He had deliberately absented himself from his wife's presence in an effort to curb his disquieting feelings toward her. Along with his suspicions and disquiet, he was now beginning to feel a degree of guilt around how he was treating everyone. Carter needed to get a grip on the situation. It would not do to allow it to go on.

He guided his horse toward the barn and made quick work of taking off his saddle and rubbing the horse down. They hadn't ridden far that afternoon, merely to check on the work being done on the fence along the perimeter. The men were making good time. The project would be done long before the snow flew. At least one thing was progressing smoothly, he was relieved to note.

His steps dragged as he approached the house, dreading facing his wife. It had been apparent his arrival had not been a welcome event for her since she had hurried back to the house as soon as he had appeared. Maybe he ought to try to learn about her from her own mouth before he heard whatever

Fred had to tell him. Then at least he would have a level of perspective. But how to get her to talk?

Taking a deep breath when he stepped into the house, Carter appreciated the clean scent that permeated the air. The smell of freshly baked bread still lingered in the air, along with what smelled like cookies of some sort. He was also surprised to note a light scent of garlic. He doubted she would put garlic in cookies, but since he didn't actually know anything about the woman, he wouldn't make any assumptions. He would try to swallow them with a smile if she truly had baked garlic flavored cookies, he told himself with a little shudder.

He could hear footsteps overhead so he headed toward the stairs but before he could climb them, he saw that she was about to descend.

"Oh," she said as she quickly stepped back from the top of the stairs. "I hadn't heard you come in."

Carter beckoned her forward. "Come down if this is where you were heading. I was only going to go up because I was looking for you."

She had started to descend when he gestured for her, but his words made her steps falter. He saw that color was rising in her cheeks, and she now looked nervous and jittery once more. Carter wished he hadn't said anything.

"Why were you looking for me?" Her voice was low, but he could hear the fear in it.

"I just wanted to ask if you were settling in all right. Have you found everything you might need?"

"Oh, yes, everything is just fine," she answered quickly, but he wondered about the truthfulness of her answer.

"If you could pick one thing that would make it feel more like home, what would you select?"

By now she was finally at the bottom of the stairs, standing in front of him. Clearly she couldn't drag out her descent any longer. She was fidgeting with the trim on her skirt and not meeting his eyes, but when his words registered with her, her head came up and she finally met his gaze. Surprise at his question was clearly written all over her face.

"Come, let us sit down. Clearly you have ideas." He laughed as her blush deepened but she didn't deny what he said. He led her over to the chairs grouped in front of the fireplace. It wasn't yet cold enough for a fire, but it was the most comfortable place to sit and talk. And he would be able to watch her closely without a table between them to hide any revealing body language.

Once they were seated, she didn't launch into speech immediately, so Carter prompted her again. "So, have you thought of something you would like?"

He could barely hear her, as her voice was so hesitant, but she finally spoke. "Curtains on the windows would make it much more homey."

Carter blinked and looked around the large room. He hadn't thought of curtains. But now that she pointed it out, he realized she was quite right. Every house he had ever been in had curtains of some sort on the windows. Even primitive mud huts usually had some sort of window covering. He almost smacked himself in the forehead. He had thought he thought of everything his house needed, but she had only been there for one day and she had already found something lacking.

"You're absolutely right. I can't believe I didn't think of it myself." He paused and looked at her closely. "Would you know how to make curtains if you had the right kind of fabric?"

Carter marvelled as her eyes lit up with delight over his question. But she didn't jump up or in any other way reveal her thoughts. She merely nodded and said, "Yes, I would. But I didn't bring much fabric with me, and I don't think Sybil will think to add it to my trunk when she sends it."

"We could go to the village mercantile tomorrow and see if they have anything you would find suitable. If they don't, we could wire your friend and ask her to send some along."

Now she finally reacted, clasping her hands together in front of her as though to restrain herself. A grin split her face, and Carter had to catch his breath over her beauty. He wished she wasn't so very beautiful.

"I would love to visit the mercantile, thank you."

"Since my house obviously needed the curtains you mentioned, that doesn't count as one thing that would make you feel more at home, so what else could you think of?"

He was surprised to see her frown.

"I don't know why you're asking me this." Her voice was soft and her confusion was obvious.

"This is going to be your home now. I don't want you to hate it." He really meant his words, even though his feelings toward her were so convoluted.

She sighed deeply and blurted out, "Books."

Carter felt his eyebrows rise toward his hairline. She obviously interpreted his surprise.

"Books would make me feel at home," she explained. "The house I grew up in was full of books."

"Did you bring any of them with you?"

She shook her head. "I only brought what I could carry. Books are too heavy. Besides they're all gone anyway."

"Your books are gone? What do you mean?"

She was back to not meeting his eyes. "It was decided that none of the books were my personal property, so I wasn't allowed to keep any of them. It was the worst loss."

Carter was confused. "I don't understand what you just said. Could you please explain it to me? You had books, but someone took them away from you?"

Ella looked as though she wished she could cut out her tongue. Regret covered her like a thick blanket, as though she didn't mean to have told him that much. She sighed softly and tried to explain, but her explanation only added to his confusion.

"When they arrived to take possession of the house, I was only allowed to keep my clothes and a small painting of me with my parents. They said everything else, including the books, belonged to my father and it couldn't be argued that it was my personal possession. I was only allowed to take my own personal things. And even then, some of my nicer gowns, they claimed could be sold, so they confiscated those as well."

Carter felt anger and confusion welling and fighting in his chest. He hated the thought of his wife being put through that. He had enough money, he could probably buy back all her things for her. He was shocked by the impulse since he had just met the woman and didn't even trust her besides.

"Why were all your things being repossessed?"

"As I said, they were deemed to be not mine, that's why they were taking them."

Carter felt his patience slipping. "Are you trying to avoid telling me the truth?"

Color flooded her cheeks. She had been pasty white while she remembered her experience, but his words brought heat back to her face. "No," she answered hotly, as though she had a temper that was rearing its head. "Why would you ask me that?"

"Well, you seem to be trying to avoid telling me what happened."

"I thought I was telling you what happened." Her forehead was furrowed into a frown. She looked as confused as he felt. Carter took a deep breath and tried to hang on to his patience.

"When all the things, except your personal possessions, were taken by someone, who was taking the things?"

"The investigators," she answered, her nose wrinkled in distaste. "And I guess the bank," she added. "The house probably ended up belonging to the bank in the end."

Carter nodded as though he understood, trying to encourage more information to continue to flow. "And who had owned the house before the bank took it?" he prompted.

"My father." Tears were welling in her eyes, and Carter had to grit his teeth to resist the urge to stop the line of questioning.

"Did he make some bad investments before his death?"

"It would seem so," she answered as the tears spilled over and trickled down her cheeks.

Carter sighed. He couldn't handle her tears. He would try again the next day if his next trip to the village didn't produce any communication from Fred.

"Never mind about all that for now. You are safe here from anyone coming to claim anything. I own everything here and don't owe anyone a single cent, so you needn't worry about a thing." Carter was slightly disgusted with himself for the need to reassure her. But he needed information before he could progress into any sort of relationship with his wife.

The smile she tried to give him was weak and watery at best, but she nodded and appeared grateful for the reprieve. "Would you like to have some dinner? I have some ham roasting in the oven."

"I thought that might be one of the delicious odors I could smell when I came in the door. Did you also bake cookies or cake or something this afternoon? It smelled delicious when I entered."

She nodded and smiled shyly. Her eyes lit up with his words as though she had never received a compliment before. She was a strange little minx, his wife.

She excused herself from his presence and returned to the kitchen. Within minutes she was calling him to the table for their evening meal. The day was finally over and Carter couldn't believe how it had alternatively flown and dragged by. There were moments that felt like hours but he couldn't believe it was suddenly bedtime. He was once again acutely aware of his wife settling in across the hallway from his bedroom. While he questioned the sanity of trying to live with her for three months without making their marriage a real one, he admitted that he couldn't really feel intimately toward her until he felt that he could trust her, no matter how beautiful she was or how wonderfully she made his house smell.

As he drifted off to sleep, he reminded himself that he needed to ask her why she looked so anxious whenever he tasted her cooking. It seemed to him as though she was insecure about her cooking skills, which was ridiculous. Everything she had cooked or baked had been delicious so far. He couldn't wait to see what she prepared for him next.

Chapter Ten

Ella stared out the window at the bright stars, chewing her lip, deep in concentration. She had been pleasantly surprised by how well the bread and cookies had turned out. Except for the very first batch of cookies, which had burnt. Thankfully with all those windows she had been able to air the house out and Carter didn't even notice. In her heart she blessed Sybil's cook once more. Her lessons had been a lifesaver. While she felt useless and restless out here in all new surroundings, it could have been much worse. At least she could feel like she was bringing some sort of value to her new husband. He certainly seemed to enjoy the food she was providing. Perhaps his own cooking had been so bad that anything was an improvement. She personally thought what she had produced wasn't half bad but she was, of course, slightly biased in her own favor. Though nothing she could do would match the accomplishments of what her own cook had been able to produce in the kitchen. Ella wished wholeheartedly for at least the hundredth time that she had descended to the kitchens a few times while she was growing up. With her new life here out West, it was obvious she had wasted her entire upbringing on skills that would serve her nothing now.

Well, except for maybe needlework. She was excited about the prospect of going to the mercantile and getting fabric for some curtains. Ella wasn't highly confident that there would be much selection so far from civilization, but anything would be better than the bareness they currently had, surely.

Ella's mind strayed back to the conversation she'd had with Carter. He had been asking her what would make her feel at home. She was surprised at the sensitive question. She hadn't thought he gave much thought to her feelings. In her experience, men expected you to be happy with whatever they gave you. She had adored her father, but even he hadn't given much thought to her or her mother's feelings. Even more than ever she realized how true that was. If he had given even the barest thought to her feelings, surely he wouldn't have left her in the situation she found herself with his death.

And now her new husband wanted to know all about it.

Ella sighed. It was foolish of her to think that she could escape her history even way out here in the back of beyond. Surely newspapers get delivered out here eventually. And letters certainly do. She had hoped that changing her name, even through marriage, would afford her a new life. But she probably owed her husband all the information she could offer him. If her trouble did follow her, he ought to know what it was.

Sighing again, Ella flopped over on the bed. She would far rather remain anonymous for a little longer. Surely he didn't need to really know anything about her past. Maybe by spring. He had said there would be little movement once winter arrived. She would tell him all about her sordid past before the end of winter.

Thus resolved, Ella punched her pillow into shape and started counting. She was drifting off to sleep before she was much past fifty, relieved to be able to put her disquieting thoughts to rest.

~~~

When the sun streaming through her uncovered window announced the arrival of morning, Ella nearly groaned aloud. Her worries had kept her up far too long the previous night. With a soft sigh she pushed the covers back and climbed down from the bed. It was remarkably comfortable. The ropes must have been recently tightened or else it hadn't been slept in since they had been done as there wasn't a single saggy area to be detected. The bedding even smelled fresh. She had a hard time imagining her husband doing the laundry, but someone must have done it. Nothing about the house had seemed unduly neglected upon her arrival. Maybe he had hired someone to come in to clean before she arrived. The thought warmed her heart and reinforced her determination to provide him a comfortable home. And she was thrilled she wouldn't have to tackle laundry any time too soon, since it appeared all had been done before her
~~~

arrival. She wouldn't be able to put it off for too long, but she dreaded the task.

She was reaching the end of her limited knowledge about cooking, unfortunately, and she had only been there a couple days. Hopefully when the rest of her things arrived from Sybil, the promised recipes and instructions would be included. Ella hoped to never have to tell her husband just how useless she really was. She had every intention of faking it until she succeeded. She would be a good wife even if the effort nearly killed her. And really, why would it kill her? Yes, it was a trifle boring. But she would just have to adjust her thinking on the matter. Her father had always said there was no excuse for boredom. That's what your mind was for. Since there were no books, maybe she could write one. Write the book she wished she could read. What an idea. Of course, there didn't seem to be anything to write it on, but perhaps she could get a notebook included in the purchase at the mercantile.

Ella felt her feet lift a little more lightly as she stepped into the kitchen. She had a plan in place for making her circumstances better. She always felt more confident with a plan. And she was going to try making oatmeal for breakfast. She had always loved oatmeal. Ella tried to keep her expectations low so as to not experience defeat, but she couldn't help her anticipation as the warm, familiar odor began to waft up from the pot.

Concentrating so as to remember all that Cook had told her, Ella didn't notice when Carter approached and so nearly jumped out of her skin when he spoke.

"You're a little jumpy in the morning, aren't you?"

Ella was fairly sure his tone was expressing amusement rather than criticism, but she felt the need to defend herself anyway.

"I was concentrating and didn't hear you."

"What were you thinking about so hard that you didn't notice me clomping around?" As he gestured toward his large size, Ella couldn't help sharing his amusement. The man surely couldn't sneak very easily.

Shrugging away her embarrassment, Ella tried to explain herself. "I'm really hungry and trying to make sure this turns out right."

"Isn't it oatmeal?" His frown indicated his confusion.

"Yes."

"Are you adding something to it that complicates it?"

"No, should I be? Do you have a particular way you prefer your oatmeal?"

Carter laughed. "No, I just don't understand how oatmeal could require concentration. Isn't it the easiest thing on earth to cook?"

Ella stood stock still and blinked at him. Anger and embarrassment warred in her chest. She reminded herself that he didn't realize he had insulted her. He had no idea that she had just learned how to cook, and that if this turned out to be edible it would be such an accomplishment. She forced her lips into a semblance of a smile.

"I also haven't had any coffee yet," she said, hoping he would just chalk it up to morning fogginess. It must have worked. Carter laughed and moved past her to where the cups sat on a shelf. Grabbing two he brushed past her again on his way to the pot. He busied himself making it once more. Ella was grateful. She still wasn't confident in her ability to brew a decent pot.

"You have it with milk, right?"

Ella was pleased he had noticed. And was surprised he was pouring for her.

"I can do that, you should sit. I can serve you."

"You're busy concentrating on the oatmeal," he replied, teasing. "And we both need some coffee. I'll be bored if I sit at the table and just wait."

Ella could see the sense of his words. Besides his boredom, she would've been mortified to have him watching her while she watched the oatmeal. With any luck, while they bustled about, the breakfast would finish itself and they could sit down to eat without him becoming any the wiser about her lack of experience.

Then she chastised herself. It probably made her the worst sort of person that she wanted to keep her secrets to herself. Maybe she ought to tell him she hadn't cooked before last week. But then she'd have to tell him all of it, and what if he wanted to be rid of her once he knew? Ella bit her lip and hoped he couldn't discern her thoughts written all over her face. She forced another bright smile to her face.

"The sun sure is bright this morning."

Carter laughed. "It's the sun. Isn't it always bright?"

Feeling like her face was burning, Ella tried to explain herself. "There isn't a single cloud in the sky and no one is burning any coal around here, so there's no dirt in the air. So I would say it's much brighter out here than it is in Boston."

His face changed then. "Well, everything's better here than it is in Boston."

Ella blinked and felt her eyebrows inch toward her hairline. "I take it you don't care much for Boston, from the tone of your voice."

"Hate the place."

Ella laughed. "Then why did you seek a wife from there?"

Carter shrugged and his smile was sheepish. "I don't hate all the people." Ella's head filled with questions as she heard the emphasis he placed on the *all* in his sentence, but he continued before she could voice any of them. "I figured it would help if we had a similar background."

"Help what?"

"Us adjust."

Ella laughed. "Do you think it worked?"

Carter shrugged again. "I don't think it was a terrible idea. And besides, there aren't any single women in these parts anyway."

Ella nodded, she could imagine that must be true. She had seen very few women on the train the further west they'd gone, and there were almost none about from what she could see of the town where the train stopped. She was distracted away from thinking on it any further by the fact that the oatmeal was finished. Or at least, she was fairly certain it was. It didn't look the same as the oatmeal her own Cook had made, but it was similar enough. She offered up a silent hope that her husband wasn't much of an oatmeal connoisseur. Thus far, he hadn't seemed to be too particular about anything she had cooked so it didn't seem that he was the fussy sort.

He scraped a little bit of sugar into his bowl and then tucked into the oatmeal with gusto. Ella tried not to be too apparent as she watched him take his first couple of bites before she even tasted it herself. She must not have been as discreet as she had hoped because suddenly he was grinning at her.

"This is the best oatmeal I've ever had."

Ella was torn between jumping with glee over his words and wondering if he was just saying that to placate her. She smiled and nodded while she scraped her own small portion of sugar into her bowl and tried it for herself.

It was far from the best *she* had ever had, but it wasn't going to kill anyone. And it wasn't terrible, if she did say so herself. But not the best. So he was either from a much less privileged background than she was or he was being kind to her sensitive feelings. Ella thought on the subject for a moment and realized she didn't really care which it was. If he were from a different background than she was, he might never find out about her past. And if he was being kind, that was a good thing. *Surely a kind husband is the type you want.*

"What are you needing to do in the village today?"

Ella was surprised to see an uncomfortable expression cross her husband's face when she asked her question. Perhaps he had forgotten he had promised to take her.

"If it's not convenient to go to the mercantile today, please don't trouble yourself. It can wait."

"Not at all," he quickly answered. "If you think the windows need coverings, we'll get some coverings. And it would be good to check on your things. We ought to send a wire to your friend to find out when we should be expecting them, so I'd like to visit the telegraph office."

Ella's heart sank. She didn't want to pester Sybil about it. It was likely Horace was giving her trouble about the expense of shipping a trunk. Ella had packed accordingly when she had decided on what to bring with her on the train, considering there was a chance nothing else would be following. She hoped her smile wasn't dimming too much. She would have to consider how to word the message so as to not cause trouble for Sybil.

"Oh no, I wouldn't want you to go to the expense of sending a telegram for me. Surely a letter would do."

"But a letter could take weeks to get an answer by the time it goes all the way there and then we await a reply. Wouldn't you want to hear back as soon as possible?"

What was there for her to do but nod in agreement? Sybil was experienced at managing Horace. If he was of a mind to give her trouble,

Sybil knew how to wind him round her finger. But despite that knowledge, Ella hated the thought of being the cause of any more trouble for her friend. Even less though did she have any wish to explain all that to her husband.

It was surprising to her just how solicitous Carter was being over her welfare. There were times she thought the man distrusted her. And he didn't seem to care too much for her company, absenting himself so often as he had over the past couple days. But now here he was offering to take her to the mercantile and the telegraph station. Perhaps she had misjudged him. Perhaps she was allowing her past experiences to color her current ones. She really ought not be so suspicious of people. She ought to view this as the fresh start it truly was and start fresh in her dealings with people. Even her husband had made somewhat of an effort to get to know her, asking her questions about what would make her feel more at home. She ought to afford him the same courtesy.

"So, what made you want to move way out here?"

Carter looked surprised by her sudden question and as though he didn't have a ready answer, which surprised her. She would have thought it would be a question he had answered many times.

"I didn't care for the superficiality of life in the city."

Ella couldn't very well fault him for that. "I can appreciate the sentiment."

Carter's eyebrows remained elevated, showing his surprise over her agreement. She felt compelled to add, "Everyone is so sweet and polite to your face but then happy to gossip about you behind your back."

"Exactly."

"But how did you pick here? Why not further west or not quite so far west?"

Carter grinned at her persistent questioning.

"I stopped in several places. And I worked for others for a time, to learn the way of things. When I was settling out here, large tracts of land could be had for barely more than putting your name on a piece of paper. When I found this spot, with its fertile soil, bounteous trees, and spectacular views, I knew I had found home. The readily available water and reasonable nearness to villages and towns also held appeal. And there were already rumors that the train would be coming through, so I knew the land would retain great value."

"You showed great foresight, then."

"My father is a businessman. Some of his instruction must have taken root in my head at some point," Carter answered with a sheepish grin.

"You are being modest. It is obvious you have worked hard and done well for yourself. You must be proud of what you have accomplished."

Carter shrugged, not agreeing with her words.

"Your father must be proud of you," she observed.

"Not especially. He wanted me to stay in Boston and take over his business, alongside my brother. He doesn't have any interest in what I'm doing out here since it is not what he had ordained for my life. My father does not like to be denied."

Ella grinned. "My father was very similar. But in the end, he's no longer here to try to enforce his wishes." Her grin felt forced. Thoughts of her father now carried bitter undertones. She didn't want Carter pursuing the thought so she hurried to turn the topic.

"How big is the village we'll be visiting? Are there many businesses and residences? Are we likely to meet many people?" While a part of Ella longed to meet people and potentially make some friends, she lived in dread of encountering anyone who might know of her disgrace.

"It's a good size for a village. Besides the mercantile, there's a rooming house, the blacksmith, the postal station, which also holds the telegraph. You won't lack for places to visit, I don't think. It's no Boston, of course, but we can get most things."

"Oh, I'm not concerned. It seems you already have most everything right here."

He offered her a smile as she rose to begin clearing the table from their breakfast. "I'll head out to speak with Brent and get the wagon ready. There's no need for you to rush but just come out when you're prepared."

Despite her misgivings, Ella couldn't help being excited at the thought of getting out of the house she hadn't left since her arrival; she used to be a gadabout in Boston. "I won't be long."

It didn't take her many minutes to clean up the few dishes they had used. She checked in the looking glass to ensure her hair was reasonably tidy even though she realized that the ride in the wagon was sure to displace it. Ella remembered the bonnets some of the women had been wearing when she arrived at the train station. She didn't own anything quite that practical. She had thought, when she had first seen them, that they were rather unattractive, but now, remembering what a tangle her hair was when she had finally arrived on Carter's land, her opinion was turned on the voluminous head coverings. If she could acquire one for herself, she would jump at the chance. And wouldn't Sybil just laugh if she could ever see her with one of those on her head, she thought with a slight pang. She pushed the thought from her mind. It would not do to become homesick. This was her home now. Sybil was a friend from her past. Yes, she was the closest thing Ella had to family, but they would stay in touch through letters. Ella's new life required her thoughts and attention. She needed to keep her focus on the bright side. She was Ella McLain now. A new life full of opportunities spread before her. ~~~

Carter tried not to let his guilt bother him as they rode toward the village. His wife's eager questions over breakfast had made him feel like a cad. She was trying to draw him out, most likely with the intention of drawing closer to him, and here he was filled with suspicions about her and trying to learn about her behind her back. Just like the Boston gossips they had spoken about. His guilty feelings were making him reticent. She had asked a few more questions as they rode along, seeming a little bit nervous about the upcoming visit to the village. He should have been reassuring her. But he had no idea how to do so. And his suspicions were seriously interfering.

Stifling a sigh, he noticed she had grown quiet when he didn't have anything to say in return. But her bright gaze was still darting around with interest. Despite his misgivings about her, he was pleased to see intelligence shining in her eyes. He hadn't thought it was a requirement in a wife, but he now realized it should have been. There would be long hours to fill over the winter. If they could have reasonable, intelligent conversations, it would certainly make the time more enjoyable. And it would bode well for any children they might be blessed with, too. He felt his face heating with the direction of his thoughts as his mind filled with his guilt once more. Here he was filled with suspicion about her, but he was thinking of having children with her. Clearly he was misguided. He was now all the more eager to reach the village. Hopefully there would be a response from Fred.

Carter was relieved when they went over the rise and the village came into view. He heard Ella's breath catch and turned to look in his wife's direction. She was obviously excited about seeing Traders Point. She cast him a smile before returning her eager gaze back to the collection of buildings that was growing before them. Turning his own gaze back toward the village, Carter tried to see it from her perspective.

It was obviously much different than Boston, but since she had been willing to leave the city, that might not necessarily be a bad thing. The dull gray of all the buildings was uninspiring, but everything was well kept and tidy despite the dirt road and clapboard of each structure. He glanced at her again. She didn't look upset or disappointed. She did look nervous, if he was correctly interpreting the expression on her face. He wondered why but didn't feel he could ask her. He turned his own attention back to the village. While it wasn't Boston, it would do; he was certain of it. There was nothing for him to be ashamed of in what he could provide his wife. Which was all the more reason for him to be certain he could be proud of his wife. Everything on the surface told him he ought to be, but he needed to settle his nagging questions. If Fred hadn't sent a message, Carter would have to question Ella himself. It was not a prospect he would look forward to, but they needed to get on with their lives, and he wouldn't be able to without his questions settled.

~~~

Ella tried to sit still, but it was almost impossible. She would have never thought she was a greedy, materialistic person. As evidence, she could point to how easily she accepted it when the investigators came in and took everything her family had owned. But here she was practically giddy at the thought of visiting the mercantile. She tried to restrain her eagerness. It was sure to be a disappointment in comparison to anything she had experienced in Boston. Undeterred, her eyes couldn't stop darting around, excited to take in everything there was to see as they approached the small cluster of buildings.

It was obvious the people of the village cared for it. Despite not being of brick and cobblestone, everything was neat and tidy. Even in Boston, Ella
~~~

had driven through neighborhoods strewn with litter, where things were falling apart, despite the houses being built of bricks. She was happy to see that it looked as though the area was thriving despite being so far from the centers of the East.

And it hadn't taken so very long to get to the village. Perhaps, once she had settled in, Carter would allow her to visit on her own if she needed to make any purchases or if she managed to make some friends she could visit. Once again Ella felt her spirits lifting. She had made the right decision when she had accepted Fred and Sybil's suggestion that she marry a stranger by proxy. Ella turned to that stranger with a grin. Her grin grew when she realized how surprised he seemed by her wide smile. She had no explanation for him so she just turned back and anticipated their approach to a mid-sized gray barn at the edge of the cluster of buildings that was the main street of the village.

"We'll leave the wagon here with the smithy while we're in the village. He doesn't mind if the horse grazes a little, and the horse will be happier here than tied to a railing by the mercantile."

"That's considerate of you," Ella commented.

Carter laughed. "Considerate of the horse, not of you."

Ella laughed with him. "Why do you say that?"

"If you buy too much, you'll have to help me carry it back to the wagon."

Ella felt the color rising in her cheeks. "I have no intention of buying much, I assure you."

"You have so little, you better reserve your judgment until you see what the mercantile has. You might just realize how much you need."

Ella held her tongue despite her intense desire to defend herself. After everything she had and lost, she strongly doubted she would ever again have trouble restraining herself while shopping. Her parents had always insisted on buying her the best of everything. She realized she had been spoiled up until six months ago. But no longer. She doubted anything the mercantile held would be a temptation to her. She returned Carter's gaze with a tight smile.

Chapter Eleven

Carter was well aware that he had misspoken in some way with her, but wasn't sure what he had said wrong. She hadn't said anything, but he had noticed when her smile dimmed and her eyes flitted away from meeting his gaze. He hadn't meant to hurt her feelings. He heaved a sigh. He would do his best to make it up to her once he had his answers.

He didn't bother acknowledging the awkward moment, merely offering her his elbow and escorting her to the front door of the mercantile.

"Take all the time you want looking around. I have to do something first, and then I'll come back and join you."

"Thank you," she answered softly as she let go of his arm and stepped slowly toward the open doorway.

Carter felt like he ought to wait for her to get settled in the store, but he also didn't want to leave her on her own for too long, so he figured he ought to get on with his business at the telegraph office.

With one more glance toward his wife, he hurried away to see if there were any messages for him.

The last sight of her lingered in his mind as he made his way to the post office. The expression on her face had been wistful as her gaze bounced around the large store. He rather thought she was surprised by the variety of things for sale at the mercantile. Even he was surprised sometimes by what was available for purchase at the store so far from a big city. The shopkeeper was obviously imaginative as he made his orders for what he would carry. Carter hoped Ella would find some things that would please her. While he couldn't quite trust her, he wanted her to be happy with her choice to come out West to a new life with him.

Carter shook his head. He was contradicting himself with each thought. He picked up his pace, hoping there was a message from Fred. His long strides ate up the distance in short order and before too many moments had passed, he was standing at the counter in the post office asking if there were any messages.

"Yes, Mr. McLain, your message has finally arrived."

Carter could barely contain himself as he snatched the sheaf of paper out of the man's hand. "Thank you," he muttered as he hurried from the office. He had noticed a bench on the way there and wanted a private place to read the note from Fred. He sank down onto the bench and his eyes scanned the few words on the page. It wasn't much of a message, and he would have to puzzle out its meaning, but he appreciated that Fred was obviously trying for discretion.

Ask to see the license.

Read Boston papers from winter/spring 1865.

That was all it said. At first Carter was confused and wondered what Fred was trying to tell him. While he appreciated his friend's discretion, a little more information would have been useful. He scanned the words again, and he finally realized what the other man was trying to get across. The license. There must be something on the marriage license. Like his wife's maiden name. He wanted to smack his own head to get some sense into it. He didn't even know his wife's name, now that he thought of it. Or at least what her name had been before she married him. Maybe Ella wasn't even her proper name.

Carter wasn't sure how he would be able to get his hands on the Boston papers from last year, but they would probably have copies of them in Town. Or maybe just finding out his wife's name would tell him some of what he wanted to know. He usually kept himself fairly well informed of what was happening in the world around him, particularly what took place in the bigger Metropolises of Boston and New York. He would ask her when they got home. Really, he should have asked her for the license right away. It had been a thoughtless oversight on his part.

~~~

Ella enjoyed the strong smell of the mercantile. There were several competing spices floating in the air. She wouldn't have thought it would be
~~~

pleasant, but it was. Taking a few deep, appreciative breaths, Ella wondered if she should experiment with some of the different spices. Cook hadn't used much other than salt and onions in her few cooking lessons, but maybe once the recipes arrived and she felt a little more confident, she could try to cook something with some of these delicious smelling seasonings.

For the time being though, she didn't want to ask Carter to buy anything other than the material he had promised her. Everything else could wait. When he had commented on her desire to buy out the store, Ella had been mortified. It was as if he knew who she was. It made her want to run and hide. Of course, it wasn't possible that he could know about her past, but she was determined not to be a financial burden on him. Material for curtains was why she was in the mercantile, and that was really all she ought to be looking at, she reminded herself as she strode across the store toward where she could see many bolts in various textures and colors.

The store had a greater variety of fabrics than she would have expected. It would be a harder decision than she had thought. She had been anticipating at most three or four options. It would have been easy had that been the case. Now she thought longingly of the stylish décor of her old home. Pushing such thoughts from her mind, she reached out to finger the most practical looking bolt of fabric she could see.

Ella was just about to seek help from the shopkeeper when she was surprised to hear someone speaking to her.

"Mrs. McLain? Is that you?"

Blinking, Ella turned to see who was calling to her and felt a wide smile spread over her face. It was the woman she had met while eating at the hotel the first day she had arrived.

"Hello. How are you? I didn't think there would be a single soul I might know in this village. How fortuitous."

Disdain seemed to fill the other woman's face for a moment before she smoothed her expression into one of pleasant inquiry. Ella assumed she must have been mistaken. The expression was there and gone in barely a blink of the eye. And there was no reason for the woman to look at her in such a way. So Ella must have imagined it. Maybe her own nerves about all the changes in her life were getting to her. She mentally shrugged.

"Isn't it just?" The other woman's smile didn't quite meet her eyes.

Ella could feel her own smile slipping. There was no way around it; the woman before her was being fake. Ella had endured her fill of such shallow relationships back in Boston. She really didn't want to engage in one now, but she also didn't want to bring trouble for herself or Carter. Speaking of him, she wished he would return. Since he already knew the woman, perhaps her strange demeanor had something to do with him.

"Are you here spending Carter's money already?"

The woman's sneer made Ella's face flame. It was her biggest fear. It was the worst accusation that could be levelled at her. She had vowed she would never again be associated with greed. It was why she had assured Carter she only wanted curtain fabric. She should have known better and stayed away from the mercantile. The stench of money must still be following her, despite having left everything behind.

"Of course, she is. And at my request, of course." The warm voice behind her nearly made her jump out of her skin with surprise, but Ella almost sagged with relief that Carter had arrived and was stepping in to save her. Ella wished wholeheartedly that she could save herself, but she wasn't sure which way to turn at this point.

She couldn't look him in the eye and knew her smile was wan as she grabbed a bolt of material without even looking.

"Are you sure about that color?" Ella could hear laughter in his voice but all she could see was the assessing glare of the other woman. She forced her gaze down to the fabric in her hands and wished a hole would open under her. He was quite right. It was purple.

She felt the side of her mouth lift up in a half smile. "Well, it would at least brighten up the place."

Ella finally looked at him and had to laugh despite the turmoil of her feelings. "No, you're right, that's not the color I meant to pick up." She quickly exchanged the bolts of fabric. The shopkeeper had materialized at Carter's elbow and appeared quite happy to help her measure out the amount she needed. It felt to Ella like an obscenely large order, but there were a large number of windows requiring coverings. She refused to look at anything else except the thread she would need to complete the project.

Carter seemed disappointed that she was disinterested in shopping, but Ella ignored both him and the other women in the store. What should have been an entertaining excursion had become a burden for her that she wished to dispense with as quickly as possible.

"Weren't you going to look at the books?"

Ella forced a laugh. "With this sewing to do, I won't have time for reading for quite a while. I'm sure we'll be back. I can look at them next time." He seemed skeptical but Ella just wanted to be free of the store and Phoebe's watchful, suspicious gaze. They hadn't spoken any further after Carter stepped in, merely nodding in farewell.

Within moments they were striding toward the wagon with the large parcel safely tucked under Carter's arm. Ella felt as though she could breathe easier as soon as they were outside.

"Would you like to look at any more shops before we head to the post office?"

"No, thank you. And I really don't think I need to send Sybil a telegram. She will send my things when she is able."

"But how will we know when we need to go to Town to collect them if we haven't had any communication with her?"

His question was reasonable, and Ella had to quit resisting his suggestion. She scrambled to think how to word the message. She was certain one paid by the word so she couldn't be chatty despite how desperately she would love to communicate with her dear friend.

Chapter Twelve

Carter frowned as he watched his wife. She was a study in contrasts. It was obvious she loved nice things. One had only to look at the clothes she had brought with her. They weren't the most practical for life on the frontier — that was for certain. They were much more decorative than what the other women of his acquaintance wore, for one thing, and of finer material. So it was obvious to him that at some point in her life she had been a shopper. But she hadn't wanted to even look around the mercantile. Perhaps she was too convinced that the village was beneath her notice as a woman of Boston. But he didn't think so. While he was still distrustful of her, it was obvious to him she was kind hearted. Her feelings had been hurt by Phoebe's implied insult that she was after his money.

He didn't know what to say to her to break the silence that had arisen between them after he had insisted they message her friend about her belongings. If she didn't want to buy anything new, she needed to get her old things. It was a matter of pride for him to take proper care of his wife.

As they strode toward the post office, Carter had another thing to concern himself about. While he had been so anxious to see if there was a message for him from Fred, it was now almost inevitable that someone would remark upon him returning so quickly. He should have waited. What was she going to think? Someone was sure to comment on his having just been there. Carter managed to restrain himself from grunting in disgust over his own stupidity. But just barely.

Of course, he was forgetting that most of the men in those parts didn't have too much to say. While the postmaster did cast him a confused expression when they first entered, not much was said. And Ella appeared far too preoccupied to notice anyway. Carter was left wondering if the woman in the mercantile had upset her that much or if she truly didn't want to message her friend. But that was ludicrous. Why wouldn't she want to contact the person she had claimed was her dearest friend? And wouldn't she want to know when her things would be arriving? He offered her what he hoped was an encouraging smile as they stepped toward the counter behind which were the telegram wires.

"Have you decided what you'd like to say?"

She bit her lip and shook her head slightly confirming to Carter that she really was nervous about the message.

"Take your time, there's no need for us to rush. Brent has everything in hand at home."

She again chewed on her lip. "I'm sorry to be a ninny about this. Have you sent telegrams before?

Is it not disconcerting that so many others might read your words? It makes it difficult to know what to say."

Again the postmaster cast a look at him, which Carter chose to ignore. Of course he'd sent telegrams before. "I know what you mean. It does make you extra careful in your wording."

She held her bottom lip between her teeth before commenting. "And isn't it more expensive if I say too much?"

"Don't let that trouble you," he quickly answered, surprised that she was again seemingly worried about his finances. "It doesn't cost so very much."

There was a small pile of paper on the counter for people to write out their messages. He could see that her hand trembled slightly as she reached for a piece and picked up the pencil. He was growing concerned for her. It was odd that she was getting so very worked up over such a little matter. He was beginning to feel that there was much she needed to confide in him.

After a few minutes of writing, scratching, and nervous fidgets, she finally handed him the paper. While she had marked a line through many of her attempts, finally at the bottom of the page was a short message. It revealed very little but would get the point across. He was impressed with her mind. She was able to boil it down into the barest necessity.

Please message when package sent.
All is well. Love, Ella.

"Will that be good enough, do you think?" she asked nervously. He had to fight the urge to put his arm around her in order to settle her nerves. He didn't think it would help her. He rather thought he was part of the problem for her nervous fidgets.

"I think it's near to perfect if you're sure you don't want to add any more details."

She shook her head vigorously. "I'll write her a letter that we can send when we come to check if there's any response in the next few days."

"Very well, then if you are certain you don't wish to do any other errands while we're in the village, we can make our way back home."

Her smile looked to be filling with relief. Carter could feel himself frowning as he wondered what was going on in her mind, and he thought of all the questions he had for her. Whatever was written on his face seemed to interrupt her expression, and her eyes widened in concern. But neither of them said anything until they were on the way, moving away from the main street.

"I never thought to ask you for our marriage certificate. It ought to be kept in a safe place." Carter had tried to think of a way to ease into the conversation but wasn't sure how to be tactful about the matter. It was the best he could do.

She blinked, clearly surprised by the topic. "It is in a safe place."

"Do you think I could see it for myself?"

Again she blinked, but her smile was wide as she nodded. "Of course. It's in my room."

Carter would have to think of an excuse to drive into Town once he had ascertained her name. Of course, if they received a message from Ella's friend that her things had been sent, he would have a ready reason. *Or you could just ask her for the information without all this subterfuge,* he reminded himself with a twinge of guilt. She seemed preoccupied, and he wondered what was on her mind.

"Do you know that woman from the mercantile very well?"

"Phoebe Crocker?"

She shrugged and nodded.

"Not terribly well. She married Jacob Crocker about two years ago. I've known Jacob for eight years, I think. I haven't spent too much time with Jacob since he got married. I will tell you, I've never had the best impression of her. I can't even tell you why, really. She seems to love to be involved in other people's business but doesn't want to share her own. It feels like she is preventing Jacob from seeing his friends. It could just be that he's preoccupied, of course. He has his own property now that he's busy looking after. We worked together before on another spread, then he hired on to my property for a while after I settled here. Now he has a small property of his own, and a wife, so I only see him at community events like weddings or funerals."

She wrinkled her nose toward the end of his explanation, and a question mark was clearly formed in her eyes. "Does everyone attend the weddings and funerals around here?"

"Sure. It's a small community. And everyone enjoys any sort of excuse to get together. The only other time we can socialize is when we get together to build someone a house or barn."

"You build each other's houses and barns?" She sounded incredulous.

"Sure, the shell of it at least. We do the best we can to get as much done in one day as possible. Then the family can manage to finish it on their own."

"That's quite wonderful," Ella commented, her wide eyes showing just how surprised she was by such an idea. "It's not like anything that would happen in the city, is it?"

Carter laughed. "Definitely not." He sobered a little and looked at her seriously while he kept the horses moving at a steady pace with a firm grip on the leads. "It's one of the reasons why I love it out here. While most people are happy to mind their own business and leave you to yours, they're also happy to lend a hand when necessary."

"Have you ever had to avail yourself of such assistance? Did the community help you build your house and barn?"

"They did. Well, the barn anyway. Most folks would've thought the house a little too outlandish to bother with. But the house where my men live used to be the main house on the property, and while I was getting help raising my first barn, there were enough people, and I had enough wood, that we were able to do the exterior of the small house, too."

He was surprised to see such a wistful expression upon her face. "I wish I had been here then to see it."

Carter chuckled. "It was a few years ago now. You would've been still a little girl, I dare say."

She didn't seem to appreciate his comment but didn't say anything further, merely offering him a tight smile and turning her attention back to the passing scenery now that they were well on the road. The silence stretched between them while Carter wondered what to say to put her at ease.

"Why did you ask about Mrs. Crocker anyway? I thought you two hit it off when you met in Town, but it didn't seem very warm when I walked into the mercantile."

Ella shrugged before answering. "I'm not really sure what happened. I wouldn't say we hit it off when we first met, but since she's the only woman I know in these parts I had actually looked forward to the possibility of running into her when I remembered that she had mentioned they didn't live too awfully far from you." She shrugged again before adding, "Perhaps she's just the moody sort."

Carter watched her as she averted her face. He thought there was probably a lot she was leaving out. It seemed to him as though the encounter had upset her. He wished he could do something to make her feel better, but he didn't yet know her well enough to know what would help. He stifled his sigh of frustration.

"Do you find it lonely out here on the frontier, far from your family and friends?"

Carter was taken aback both by the question and by her tone. He rather thought she sounded lonely.

"Are you starting to feel homesick?"

To his surprise, she shrugged as though it didn't matter to her one way or the other. He wondered if he ought to question her about it but to his further surprise, she continued speaking after a brief pause.

"I don't have any family left back in Boston. My mom was an only child and her parents have already passed. My father was estranged from his family, so I don't know them. And all but one of my friends proved not to actually be a friend. So any homesickness I might feel is for something that no longer exists." She cleared her throat delicately and offered him a bright smile that didn't quite make it to her eyes. "It would have been nice to make some women friends in the area, but I think it best if I stick to animals for now. I know I have to wait until spring for a kitten, but tell me a little bit more about the lambs. I know they probably wouldn't work too well as an indoor pet, but surely it wouldn't hurt for me to befriend them."

Carter laughed and started talking, telling her more about why he was raising sheep on a cattle ranch and enjoying the sun on his shoulders as they made their way home. The time flew and he appreciated her intelligent questions. Even though she obviously knew little about rural life, she was interested and was able to formulate insightful questions, stimulating a lively conversation. He'd never had such an in depth conversation about his methods and plans for the spread. His appreciation for the woman at his side grew along with his pride in himself. Her softly uttered, "You've done so well for yourself," were the best words he'd ever heard.

As they chatted the rest of the way home and even through the evening after he had finished his chores, at the back of his mind Carter was wondering why they were able to converse so freely and yet his wife never ended up telling him anything of import about herself. He realized he ought to try harder to engage her in sharing personally, but he was enjoying her company far too much to disrupt their flow at this point.

Chapter Thirteen

Eleanor St. Clair. Now he knew her name prior to becoming his wife. And with the name came her public history. He didn't even need to ask her if her father was Winston St. Clair. Fred wouldn't have mentioned the newspaper articles if there were nothing of note about her name. Ella had handed him the folded paper that was their marriage license within moments of arriving home. Her face had been a study in nonchalance, but that very fact revealed to him how very much she was affected by the need to share that information with him. Up until that point, there had been an almost perpetual smile or grin on her face since she had awoken from her faint on the train platform in Town. Carter wasn't sure if the smiles were real or not, but the fact that there wasn't one gracing her lovely face now told him how very seriously she took the matter. That was why he had waited until she had left the room before he unfolded the paper. He had been nervous to learn the truth.

He knew enough about life to realize that whatever he had read about her scandalous father wasn't the full truth. It certainly wouldn't be her truth. And it didn't mitigate the fact that the poor woman had been all alone after the bottom had dropped out of her world. What it did explain to a certain extent was why such a beautiful young woman was willing to accept their arranged marriage. And he had been right. Knowing that did make all the difference to him. Now that he knew, he realized it wasn't so very bad. He strongly doubted she had been involved in her father's dishonest schemes. He accepted it had been foolish on his part to arrange for a wife to be sent to him without looking into her background before making it legal. It could have been so much worse. Of course, he had trusted Fred.

He could see that Ella was brave for accepting his offer rather than conniving. While it could be argued that not telling him such an important piece of information was being dishonest, Carter could see that it would be difficult for her to trust him with it while she didn't yet know him. He could only imagine what kind of treatment she had received from the authorities and her former acquaintances when her father's fraudulent activities had come to light. The fact that she had not been arrested told him the authorities did not consider her in the least involved. He thought she was rather fortunate that she hadn't been thrown into jail just because people thought someone should pay for Mr. St. Clair's crimes. Since he was no longer around to take the blame, his daughter could have very well been considered an easy target.

This thought made his chest ache for his wife. He wished she would tell him all about it. Carter didn't like to think about his own time living in Boston, and it was only that he didn't feel he fit in. He hated to think of her experiences, but he did wish she would confide in him. He was certain she must be scarred from them, and surely talking about them would help. Didn't women always want to talk things out?

~~~

Carter sat atop his horse and stared off into the distance. He truly loved his piece of Iowa. He loved that, from this vantage point, all he could see was his own land. He loved how lush and green it was for most of the year. He loved how fertile it was and how relatively easy it was to cultivate his herd. And he really appreciated the fact that one would have to ride for a while before finding another person who wasn't affiliated with him. The closest neighbor was at least a twenty-minute hard ride away. He loved that. But it might not be considered a positive for his wife. She probably wanted company and social interaction. Carter sighed. He was going to have to go to Boston to clear his wife's name. His gut clenched at the thought.

It had been almost two weeks since he had taken the folded marriage license from his wife's trembling hand. He was well aware of the fact that she was wondering whether or not he had recognized her name. He could tell from the way she watched him from the corner of her eye while she stood at the stove or the way she tried to be nonchalant as she asked him if he ever read the newspapers. She had tried to be subtle about it,
~~~

asking if it was hard to come by the news in these parts. He had kept his face straight as he answered her that while the papers were out-dated when they arrived, they did get to keep up on the goings on of the world.

Carter watched the cattle grazing, but his mind was back at his house. He felt a surge of guilt when he thought about how he had left her hanging for so long. He couldn't fault her for not telling him her history if he hadn't been willing to tell her that he now knew her history. He ought to have set her mind at ease, assuring her that he knew and that it wasn't a problem for him. Because, really, how could it be? They were legally bound to one another anyway. And one couldn't choose one's relatives. Look at his. He would have rather had a warm, loving family instead of the harsh, demanding father he had grown up with. In Carter's opinion, it was what you did with yourself once you were no longer under the control of your family that was the important thing. And all he could see about his wife was how beautifully she was adjusting to life on the frontier.

She was a wonderful cook. Not terribly imaginative as she was repeating the same things over and over, but that was probably due to her lack of experience. What she did know how to cook was delicious. Perhaps he ought to send away for a cookbook for her. Of course, she might find that insulting. Or perhaps not. From what he had learned about her so far, she wasn't actually one to take offense easily. Her easy-going nature was one of the things he found most attractive about her.

While it was true, if you only looked at her you could get distracted by her outward beauty, and he certainly had been when she first arrived. And he realized that three weeks wasn't a terribly long acquaintance. But now that he had gotten used to looking at her, he had been able to see beneath the surface.

He enjoyed watching her concentrate while she cooked. It always made him want to laugh a little bit, but he admired the effort she was putting in. She had probably never had responsibility for a meal before.

He appreciated her questions about his land and why he had moved to the frontier. She had a keen mind and was making an effort to settle in rather than wallowing in the tragedies she had endured. From the beginning he had wondered if her constant smile was genuine or a front. He had finally concluded that it was a little of both. Most of the time he was quite certain her smiles were genuine, but there were times that he was sure she was smiling in an effort to convince herself, rather than him, so he didn't consider it to be a form of dishonesty.

He remembered almost fondly the incident of the coffee. The coffee had been dreadful. But that's when he knew he was falling for her and he didn't care about who her father had been. Up until three days ago, he had been the one making the coffee before each meal. It had become a routine for them. He enjoyed being in the kitchen with her. The little frown of concentration she couldn't quite hide made him want to put his arms around her. It was becoming harder and harder to resist.

But he had been held up in the barn with some sort of chore. He couldn't remember what it had been. Whatever it was, he was delayed arriving in the house and she had finished her preparations and so had tried to make the coffee. There she was frowning over the pot when he arrived. Carter was shocked how disappointed he was that their little ritual was to be disturbed that day. And then they had sipped the brew. Ella had run to the sink and spit it out, but he had made a valiant effort to swallow it down. He hadn't even realized at first that she was crying. When he glanced over to where she was standing in the kitchen, giant tears were flowing silently down her cheeks and she looked as though her world had collapsed.

Without thought, Carter was across the room with her in his arms. She had sobbed pitifully for several moments, mumbling almost incoherently into his dampening shirt.

"I thought I could do it. You always make it look so easy. And Cook said it wasn't hard. But I just can't do it. Maybe I'll never succeed. I'm the worst wife in history."

Rubbing circles on her back, Carter had assured her that she was far from the worst wife and while she would surely learn how to make coffee, he didn't mind making it himself.

"But I'm the cook here," she had insisted. "I should be able to do it."

"You'll learn," he had assured her once more. "But I promise, I like doing it."

That finally got through to her and her tears slowed. Once the violence of her storm of tears was easing, Carter had become aware of how perfectly she fit in his arms. Her head came to just below his chin while she was huddled into him so he could comfortably rest his chin on her bent head. She was slight but he could tell she was perfectly rounded in all the right places. He had been well aware that she was a beautiful woman but hadn't really thought about the practicalities of having her in his arms. He quite liked it. He had to fight the urge to tighten his arms further around her. Carter reminded himself sharply that he was trying to comfort, not seduce, her. There were still two months to go for that.

But that was when he had realized he had already given her his heart. Even though he knew her background, he also knew that it did not define her. She was the most intelligent woman he had ever come across. And for all the trials she had faced, this was the first time he had seen her express a negative emotion. He marveled at her sunny disposition.

Carter sighed. He was mooning around about the woman like a love struck teen-aged boy. He needed to figure out a way to tell her that he knew who she was and explain why he had waited to say anything. And he had to accept that he needed to take her back to Boston. He didn't think she would be happy about it. While she seemed to be a little sad or lonely from time to time, he didn't have the impression she was pining for the city. But what she had faced didn't sit right with him. He needed to help her regain her position. His father would be thrilled to have him back. It made Carter's stomach turn, but there was nothing to do but face it.

With another deep, heartfelt sigh Carter allowed his gaze to finally focus, and he looked around. He had ridden up here to this hill for the beauty and solitude to soothe him as he firmed up his decision. He could see some of his men in the distance. They would be able to keep watch over the herd. He wasn't needed here. He squeezed his legs to get his horse moving again. It was time to head to the house and talk with his wife.

~~~

Ella stared sightlessly out the window, her mind churning with restless thoughts. It had been two weeks since she had handed the marriage license to Carter. Two weeks of wondering if her maiden name meant anything to him. Wondering if or when he would realize who she had been.

Her heavy sigh sounded despondent even to her own ears. She ought to try to talk to him about it even though the thought of discussing her background made her stomach clench with nerves. The man said he read the papers, he couldn't have possibly missed the biggest scandal to have hit Boston in years. It had been front page news for weeks up to and including her parents' deaths. The very worst headline Ella had seen felt seared into her mind: *Crooked Shipping Magnate Slaughters Wife and Self.* She shivered as she remembered it. There was no doubt she shouldn't have read the article, but she hadn't been able to help herself. It was a far more salacious headline than the facts of the matter had proven to be. It had been a carriage accident. Her father had certainly not slaughtered her mother. But even to Ella's inexperienced mind, she had to think it would take some effort to make
~~~

the horses drive off a cliff. From what she was learning about the large animals here on the frontier, they were far more intelligent than she had ever realized. And they were quite capable of seeing in the dark. But they were also obedient. So she could see how the investigators might think the accident had been deliberate.

Of course, the fact that her parents had taken luggage with them lead Ella to think they were perhaps merely trying to run away from their problems, even temporarily, rather than trying to take their own lives. But there was no way she could convince the papers to print a retraction. Even if they had agreed to do so, it certainly wouldn't have been on the front page. And the lawyer she had consulted had been unwilling to even consider a defamation suit against the paper. He had said there weren't enough facts supporting her version of things and even though the word choices in the headline were inflammatory, he didn't think they could be proven to be slanderous. Ella was pretty sure the man just thought she didn't deserve any restitution. The investigators probably would've claimed any monies she might have gained as part of her parents' estate anyway.

Ella tore her gaze from the window to look around the room. She had gotten lucky in the end anyway. She was far from Boston and had a comfortable roof over her head. She just wished she could feel secure in her setting. Her uncertainty was starting to drive her batty.

Ella glanced back at the window. More specifically, the window dressings she had created. She knew pride was considered a sin, but she couldn't help how very proud of herself she was over the silly things. It was the brightest highlight of the past two tiresome weeks. As a properly bred young woman of Society, she had been trained since she was old enough to hold a needle and thread to do needlework. She was relieved to note that she had been able to take that skill and apply it to something more practical than embroidering her initials on a handkerchief. She had been hard-pressed not to preen when Carter had noticed the new curtains. It was a lovely memory.

Carter had been sitting enjoying his first cup of coffee while she had been finishing off toasting the bread when he suddenly spoke. Ella had managed not to burn herself as she quickly retrieved the bread she had dropped onto the stovetop.

"You've finished the curtains," he had exclaimed. "When did you hang them? I didn't even notice."

Ella had felt shy as she turned and grinned at him. "I hung those yesterday afternoon."

"So I sat through supper and didn't notice?" He was incredulous. "I didn't think I was that unobservant."

Ella laughed. "With the days getting shorter, it wasn't very bright in here when you came in."

"Still, I should've noticed. You did a great job."

Embarrassed, Ella tried to deflect his praise. "Don't look too closely or you'll see that I didn't."

"Well, they look great to me. Thank you for doing that. You were right, that was the something missing from this room."

Ella's face began to hurt from how wide her grin was. She couldn't restrain her delight over his compliment.

It had been a short interlude, probably meaning very little to Carter, but the memory warmed Ella whenever she thought of it, which was every time she walked through the room. She still had the windows on the second floor to finish, but she was very happy with how this floor had turned out.

Ella returned to the kitchen, thinking about Carter as she went. She had a hankering for a cup of coffee but felt that was firmly still his task to perform. She remembered fondly the comfort he had offered her over the incident when she had tried to make the brew. What a disaster! But despite how mortified she was, it was the most relaxed she had felt in the weeks since she'd lived there. Crying had released some of her pent up anxieties. It had been so kind of him to offer her comfort despite her mishap in the kitchen.

Prior to that, she had always wondered what would happen if he found out what a fraud she was. She was just like her father, just on a different scale. Ella was feeling worse and worse each day. She should have told him the full story when she met him. Now she feared losing him if he were ever to find out. The anxiety of it all was going to eat a hole in her stomach.

Carter was such a kind, honest person, she thought. He had been quite open with her about his family background. When he had told her about his childhood poverty but then his father's sudden wealth, it helped her to better understand why he was so determined to make a success of his spread out here in Iowa. And also why he wanted to succeed on his own terms, not his father's. He had told her those things, but she had never told him about her family. And she dreaded the moment if he ever found out. Surely he would want to disown her then. It was all the more reason why she had to make herself invaluable to him. If she made his home more comfortable than it had ever been, surely he would be reluctant to cast her off.

Chapter Fourteen

There was a knock at the door, startling Ella just as she was opening the oven. A slight frown marred her forehead as she pulled the cookies out before hurrying to the door. She hadn't heard a knock on the door since she'd lived there. Only she or Carter ever came to the house. The men who worked for her husband seemed to always seek him out while he was out of doors. She could hear a dog barking in the distance, perhaps in response to the knocking. As Ella rushed toward the second rap on the door, it crossed her mind that it was rather strange that the ranch hands never came to the house. Then fear seized her. A knock at the door had heralded terrible news for her in the past. Her steps slowed. But the third knock, this time even more vigorous, pushed her feet closer to the door. With a deep breath, she pulled it open.

It took her a moment to recover. And then surprise and trepidation in equal measures spread through her.

"Mrs. Crocker, what a surprise."

"Mrs. McLain," the other woman acknowledged with barely a smile.

"Won't you come in?" Ella had to ask for politeness' sake. Just as the words were done falling from her lips, Carter rounded the corner of the house.

"The dogs let me know we had company," he said. To Ella it seemed that his smile was tighter than usual. But that might be because she had been on tenterhooks around him for more than a week. She was finally to the point that she didn't trust herself to judge his expressions.

"I was just about to put the kettle on for some tea, and the cookies just came out of the oven, why don't you join us ladies?"

"Very well. Thank you."

Ella's stomach was clenched tight. She would much rather be working on the window dressings than drinking tea with Phoebe Crocker, but she stifled her sigh. There was nothing else she could have done with the woman standing on their front porch. Surprisingly, the woman's sour expression transformed as soon as Carter had arrived on the scene, although she still hadn't said anything. That all changed though as soon as they stepped inside. Ella stepped to the kitchen to boil the water for tea, and Carter steered their guest to the chairs in the sitting area.

"It's so kind of you to take time away from your busy schedule to say hello, Carter." The woman's breathy voice made Ella grit her teeth. If she wasn't certain the woman knew Carter was married, Ella would think she was flirting with her husband.

"It's not every day we get visitors. No one should be so busy they can't take a few minutes to share a cup of tea with a neighbor."

The woman let out a trill of laughter that grated on Ella's nerves. She almost dropped the pot she was arranging as she glanced over in time to see Mrs. Crocker's hand tightly gripped on Carter's forearm. The only comfort she took was in the fact that Carter didn't look terribly pleased with the turn of events. His gaze rose to meet hers.

"Do you need a hand in there, Ella?"

"Don't be silly, Carter, kitchen work is for women. You just sit down here comfortably with me and tell me how you've been keeping. You haven't come by for a visit in ages."

Ella couldn't believe the other woman's behavior. She was prevented from stomping over there and wrenching the dreadful woman away from Carter by the fact that he looked so uncomfortable. He clearly wasn't encouraging the terrible behavior.

As quickly as she could, Ella plated the cookies and assembled the tea, loading everything on a tray she had found in the larder. Before too much time had passed, she joined the other two in the sitting area.

"How do you take your tea, Mrs. Crocker?" she asked as solicitously as she could manage.

"With milk and sugar," came the cool response.

Ella barely blinked over the difference in how the woman was reacting to her in comparison to how she was treating Carter. But she did wonder if the woman was of sound mind. This prompted some sympathy from her. If the poor dear was senile, one must make allowances.

"Cookie?" she asked with a smile.

"I doubt you would know how to bake properly," Mrs. Crocker answered without bothering to look at her. Ella was shocked. Even in Boston, all the bad things said about her had been behind her back. She had never had someone be quite that rude to her very face.

"I beg your pardon?"

"You needn't beg my pardon, it's your husband's you ought to be begging. Does he even know what a dreadful bargain he struck in marrying you?"

Ella was stuck silent by the woman's words and sank shakily into the chair she was nearest to. Before she had gathered her wits, Carter was speaking.

"I think you ought to explain yourself, Mrs. Crocker. It is only my long time friendship with your husband that is preventing me from throwing you out of the house without an explanation. This is my wife's home, and I will not allow anyone to speak to her in such a disrespectful manner."

"Oh Carter, you are so kind and gracious. I only spoke thusly because I am so very angry at how you have been taken in by this terrible girl. If only you had waited for my sister to arrive for a visit. You would have seen what a lovely wife she would make you."

Ella's worst fears were coming to fruition right before her eyes. She should have told Carter everything the moment she had stepped off the train. Or at the very least, on the drive from

Council Bluffs to their home. Now it was all going to be revealed in the worst possible way by this shrew. Ella couldn't imagine how the dreadful person even knew about her, let alone what business she thought it was of hers to inform Carter about it. Then she remembered. Of course, she had wanted Carter to marry her sister. So she was predisposed against Ella. All it had taken was a fast moving letter home or even a telegram if she was in that much of a hurry, and she would have been able to find out everything. Ella just prayed she didn't shed a tear in front of Mrs. Crocker. She didn't want to give her the satisfaction. While she wanted to run screaming from the room, Ella lifted her chin and stared at the woman, affronted that she would so viciously speak of her right in front of her but without speaking to her. She shifted her gaze to her husband to try and gauge his reaction

Carter looked shocked. Ella averted her eyes. She couldn't bear to watch his face as her life disintegrated before her.

His voice was calm and low. "My wife is not a terrible girl, and I have not been taken in by her in any way. I do believe it is time for you to be going. Please, don't return unless you are in the company of your husband. I don't think he would appreciate hearing how you are carrying your slander around the community."

Ella could see that Carter's mention of her husband seemed to give Mrs. Crocker pause, but it didn't dissuade her from her mission.

"You are being deceived, Carter. I could not keep it to myself, you had to be warned. Her father was a thief and a murderer, and she's probably here to swindle you from all your hard earned gains. Since your marriage was arranged in such a shady manner, it probably wouldn't be too terribly difficult to have it dissolved. Then you would be free to marry my dear sister."

"You are the one who is deceived. I would never have married your sister. And you don't know the first thing about my wife."

"Oh, but I do, Carter. Immediately after you introduced us in Council Bluffs, I went and wired home to Boston. It took some doing, but I was able to track down her history. Surely you couldn't have known about it or you wouldn't have married her. I just got the full story yesterday and had to come tell you about it today. I can get you whatever proof you might want. And I'm quite sure it could be grounds for annulling the marriage as surely she has committed fraud against you by marrying you under false pretences."

Carter stood, towering over the crazed woman. "You have spoken quite enough. I will not listen to you uttering another word about my wife. You can be sure Jacob will be hearing about this. Please, leave by your own power. I would dislike having to physically remove you, but I will do it if you are not gone from this house within the next five minutes."

"But Carter, don't allow yourself to be fooled by her physical beauty. She is rotten on the inside."

Carter's voice got even quieter. "You're now questioning my sense? You have gone beyond the bounds. My wife is not the rotten one in this room." He grabbed Mrs. Crocker's arm, ignoring her gasp of dismay, and hustled her to the door. Putting her outside, Carter slammed the door behind her. Silence followed the solid thud of the heavy door making contact with the doorframe. In the distance, a dog started barking again.

Chapter Fifteen

Carter was amazed at how poised Ella had been during Phoebe's diatribe. But as he watched her, her composure slowly crumpled. He could see tears fill her eyes even though she obviously was trying to restrain them.

"I think I need to lie down," she said softly through trembling lips. Without waiting for him to reply, she lifted her skirt in one clenched fist and ran up the stairs, shutting the door to her room with a quiet click. Carter would have preferred if she had slammed that door.

He should have talked to her about what he knew. He should have realized news like this wouldn't stay completely hidden, even here on the frontier. He just wouldn't have expected it to arrive this quickly. But he wouldn't allow shrewish women like Phoebe Crocker to gossip and slander his wife. He stood for some moments staring out the window before his gaze focused on the curtains hanging on either side. He was stunned to feel a smile stretching his lips at a time like this. She had managed to hang more of the curtains she had been working on.

Carter softly knocked on her door. Part of him hoped she had cried herself to sleep, for he was certain she had retreated to her room for the privacy to weep. Perhaps if she were able to sleep for a few minutes, she would be able to awaken with a better perspective of this afternoon's debacle. There was a rustle of fabric telling him she was not asleep, but she didn't say anything.

Opening the door slightly, Carter put his head into his wife's room. He didn't wish to violate her privacy, but he couldn't leave this matter to rest.

He spotted her lying face down on the bed. She lifted her tearstained face upon his entrance.

"Can I come in?"

His heart nearly broke as she valiantly tried to pull the tatters of her composure around herself. She nodded as she sat up and tried to smooth back her hair. It was usually tied back tightly as though she had exerted her will upon it, but now unruly curls were springing out all over her head as though even her hair were expressing its distress over the situation.

Before he had a chance to say anything, even as he was approaching the side of the bed, thinking to take a seat, she burst into speech.

"I never should have kept my background a secret from you, Carter. I'm so terribly sorry. Do you think if I leave you'll be able to salvage your reputation within the community?"

"What?" he demanded much more harshly than he intended.

Her face flushed, and more tears leaked from the corners of her eyes but she did not cower away.

"I said, if I leave, no one should hold my past against you. You'll be able to retain your position within the community."

"My position within the community is perfectly safe, I can assure you."

"But Mrs. Crocker said—"

"I don't care what that tart said," Carter interrupted forcefully. "She doesn't control anything around here, certainly not people's opinions."

"But if she tells everyone about me, that's sure to affect their opinions." Carter hated how sad her voice sounded.

"It cannot be avoided that if she spreads her tales around, some will be affected by it, but I promise you, the people around here think for themselves. They will allow you to prove yourself for yourself. And most are predisposed to think well of others. Most have their own reasons for starting new lives out here. And they all have a healthy dose of skepticism for whatever Phoebe Crocker might have to say."

Ella sniffled and then wiped her nose delicately with a handkerchief. She took a deep breath and looked so beautiful in all her rumpled devastation that Carter's heart broke just a little bit on her behalf. It was obvious she was trying so hard to be brave.

"It's kind of you to say that, Carter, but the fact is, she wasn't lying. If anyone finds out what my name was before I married you and then they take the effort to read any old newspaper articles, they'll know the terrible truth about me. I did take advantage of you by accepting Fred's proposition of marriage. My father was a crook. And I don't know how they died for sure. Maybe he *was* a cowardly murderer." Her lips trembled, but she continued on. "You should let me go and then you can marry some respectable woman. I really don't think you should align yourself with anyone connected to Mrs. Crocker, but you deserve a better partner than me."

"No," Carter declared. "There isn't a better partner for me than you, so you're going to have to stick with me."

Her smile was tremulous and she looked relieved at his words, but she still shook her head. "But you don't even know. She said some nasty things, but you don't actually know what my background is. When you hear all about it, you'll agree with her."

"No, I won't. And I already know. I knew when you gave me the wedding license. As soon as I saw your maiden name, I knew who your father must have been. And it doesn't matter. While I would have rather you had told me yourself, and I would still like to hear the details from you, since I think it would do you good to discuss it, your background doesn't matter to me except from the standpoint of how it must hurt you to know what your parents when through. And everyone turning their backs on you. People like Mrs. Crocker, who are in no position themselves to point any fingers, let me tell you."

Ella was looking at him with wide eyes, amazement written all over her face, as though she didn't know whether to believe him or not.

"Pack your bags, we're going to the train station."

With a blink her face crumpled and her tears resumed flowing. Carter thought back to his last words and quickly retracted them.

"I'm not sending you away. I mean we're both going. I'm going to pack my bags, too."

Ella blinked at him, looking a little like a baby owl with her curls every which way in a halo around her head.

"Then where are we going? We cannot run away from what Mrs. Crocker is saying. Your beautiful house and property are here."

"We're not running away, we're going back to face your history. We'll go to Boston and force that dreadful society to retract their words and views of you."

Carter's stomach turned over at the thought of what he'd just said, but he was certain it was the best thing to do for his wife. From the looks of her, she had been at the center of Boston society and had no doubt been devastated by being cast out.

He was shocked when a loud peel of laughter slipped from between her lips. Perhaps the stress had turned her mind slightly. He reached out and grasped one of her hands. She was waving the other in front of her face as though she were trying to wipe away her mirth but was having trouble regaining control of it.

"I'm so sorry, Carter, I hope you don't think me dreadfully rude for laughing over your suggestion. I know you made it with the best possible intentions, but there is really no need to make such a sacrifice."

"Any sacrifice is worth the effort if it will make you happy."

"Oh, that is so sweet of you to say, and I promise you I am comforted by your words, but this particular sacrifice would be needless. We *both* hate Boston society. I wouldn't want you to make that effort for me. Why would I want to be restored into the good graces of the type of people who would shun me for something outside of my control? And who would send word of my misfortunes to follow after me so that I cannot start fresh?"

There was a space of silence while they both assessed each other, as though questioning each other's sincerity. Carter couldn't believe he was being granted a reprieve. His offer to return to Boston had been sincere, but he was thrilled to hear she was disinterested in accepting.

"If you meant it when you said you want me to remain at your side and you truly don't think my presence will damage you, this is exactly where I'd like to remain."

Carter's heart swelled and he got to his feet, pulling her up and encircling her in his arms.

~~~

Ella had been so comforted by his words and Carter's warm grasp on her hand but was surprised when he pulled her into his arms as he
~~~

got to his feet. He was able to maneuver her easily, as though she weighed nothing. His strength was one more thing to find attractive. The butterflies that seemed to be omnipresent whenever Carter was around resumed fluttering in her midsection.

"Ella McLain, I know we might have gotten off to a rather shaky start. You are probably still grieving and you have been trying so hard to hide how little experience you have with anything that is normal life here on my spread. Your bravery has been a source of wonder for me ever since I realized how unprepared you must have felt for our life out here."

She hadn't expected such warm words from him. Ella could feel the prickle of tears behind her eyelids but she blinked rapidly, not wanting to spoil the moment with tears and wanting to watch his face closely as he said such lovely things. Before she could say anything in response, Carter resumed speaking.

"When you first arrived, I fell a little bit in love with your outward beauty. I was stunned that such a beautiful woman could be mine. But then the very shallowness of my immediate reaction led me to be suspicious of why such a lovely woman would need to accept an offer of a proxy marriage. I'm sorry if my wayward thoughts caused you even a moment of pain or sadness. As the time passed, I realized you couldn't be anything other than what I saw, a genuine, lovely, young woman who had fallen into tough times but had accepted an offer of assistance. You worked hard to make my life comfortable, preparing delicious meals, washing the laundry, beautifying my house, taking on tasks that had to be unfamiliar to you, without a single word of complaint."

"Oh, Carter, you needn't say such things to me, I'm so grateful to you for saving me from my troubles."

"But don't you see? You're the one who has saved me. I didn't even realize how lonely and cantankerous I had become. Your arrival has changed everything. The only thing I can be proud of is that I was right, a wife from Boston was exactly right for me, but only the right wife, you."

Finally, Ella couldn't stem the flood of her tears. She was touched to the deepest part of her heart by his words. Her own heart swelled with love toward him. Her smile widened as his head dipped toward hers. He was going to kiss her. She could hardly stand still, she was so giddy with joy. But then his lips covered hers, and she was swept away in a tide of sensation. She had never felt so happy in her life. She just knew they were going to live happily ever after.

The End

Be sure to read the next *Married by Proxy* book

A Wife for Ransom

What happens when they realize how very permanent their proxy marriage truly is?

About the Author

I've been writing pretty much since I learned to read when I was five years old. Of course, those early efforts were basically only something a mother could love ☺ I put writing aside after I left school and stuck with reading. I am an avid reader. I love words. I will read anything, even the cereal box, signs, posters, etc. But my true love is novels.

Almost ten years ago my husband dared me to write a book instead of always reading them. I didn't think I'd be able to do it, but to my surprise I love writing. Those early efforts eventually became my first published book – *Tempting the Earl* (published by Avalon books in 2010). There were some ups and downs in my publishing efforts. My first publisher was sold and I became an "orphan" author, back to the drawing board of trying to find a publishing house. It has been a thrilling adventure as I learned to navigate the world of publishing.

I believe firmly that everyone deserves a happily ever after. I want my readers to be able to escape from the everyday for a little while and feel upbeat and refreshed when they get to the end of my books.

When not reading or writing, I can be found traipsing around my neighborhood admiring the dogs and greenery or travelling the world with my favorite companion.

Stay in touch:

Website: www.wendymayandrews.com

Facebook: www.facebook.com/WendyMayAndrews

Instagram: www.instagram.com/WendyMayAndrews

Twitter: www.twitter.com/WendyMayAndrews

www.ingramcontent.com/pod-product-compliance
Lightning Source LLC
Chambersburg PA
CBHW030959210726
48290CB00007B/2378